GENTLEMEN OF THE ROAD

MICHAEL CHABON

Waterstone's

SCEPTRE

GENTLEMEN OF THE ROAD

In the Caucasus Mountains around AD 950, two
wandering adventurers and unlikely soul mates live as they
please and survive as they can – as blades and thieves for
hire and practised bamboozlers. Until, following a bloody
coup in the Jewish empire of the Khazars, they get
dragooned into the service of a fugitive prince, who
burns to reclaim his throne . . .

Summoning the spirit of *The Arabian Nights* and
The Three Musketeers, this is a novel brimming with action,
raucous humour, cliff-hanging suspense, and a cast of
colourful characters worthy of Scheherazade's most
tantalising tales.

ALSO BY MICHAEL CHABON

The Mysteries of Pittsburgh
A Model World and Other Stories
Wonder Boys
Werewolves in Their Youth
The Amazing Adventures of Kavalier & Clay
Summerland
The Final Solution
The Yiddish Policemen's Union

GENTLEMEN
OF THE ROAD

ILLUSTRATED BY GARY GIANNI

SCEPTRE

First published ～～～ ～ain in 2007 by Sceptre
An im～～～～～～～ & Stoughton
An ～～～～～～ ～K company

First published in ～～～～ ～es in 2007 by Del Rey
An imprint of Random House, Inc

I

A CIP catalogue record for this title is available from the British Library

ISBN 978 0 340 95354 9

Printed and bound by Clays Ltd, St Ives plc

Hodder & Stoughton policy is to use papers that are natural, renewable and
recyclable products and made from wood grown in sustainable forests. The
logging and manufacturing processes are expected to conform to the
environmental regulations of the country of origin.

Hodder & Stoughton Ltd
A division of Hodder Headline
338 Euston Road
London NW1 3BH

www.hodder.co.uk

To Michael Moorcock

Despising all my glory, abandoning my high estate, leaving my family, I would go over mountains and hills, through seas and lands, till I should arrive at the place where my Lord the King resides, that I might see not only his glory and magnificence, and that of his servants and ministers, but also the tranquility of the Israelites. On beholding this my eyes would brighten, my reins would exult, my lips would pour forth praises to God, who has not withdrawn his favor from his afflicted ones.

—*letter of* HASDAI IBN SHAPRUT,
*minister of the Caliph of Spain, to Joseph,
ruler of Khazaria, circa 960*

"From now on, I'll describe the cities to you," the Khan had said, "in your journeys you will see if they exist."

—ITALO CALVINO, *Invisible Cities*

CONTENTS

CONTENTS

CONTENTS

ILLUSTRATIONS

GENTLEMEN OF THE ROAD

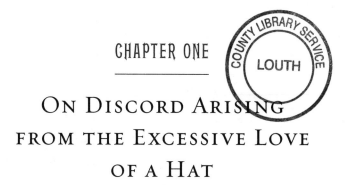

CHAPTER ONE

On Discord Arising
from the Excessive Love
of a Hat

For numberless years a myna had astounded travellers to the caravansary with its ability to spew indecencies in ten languages, and before the fight broke out everyone assumed the old blue-tongued devil on its perch by the fireplace was the one who maligned the giant African with such foulness and verve. Engrossed in the study of a small ivory shatranj board with pieces of ebony and horn, and in the stew of chickpeas, carrots, dried lemons and mutton for which the caravansary was renowned, the African held the place nearest the fire, his broad back to the bird, with a view of the doors and the window with its shutters thrown open to the blue dusk. On this temperate autumn evening in the kingdom of Arran in the eastern foothills of the Caucasus, it was only the two natives of burning jungles, the African and the myna, who sought to warm their bones. The precise origin of the African remained a mystery. In his quilted gray bambakion with its frayed hood, worn over a ragged white tunic, there was a hint of former service in the armies of Byzantium, while the brass eyelets on the straps of his buskins suggested a sojourn in the West. No one had hazarded to discover whether the speech of the known empires, khanates, emirates, hordes and kingdoms was intelligible to him. With his skin that was lustrous as the tarnish on a copper kettle, and his eyes womanly as a camel's, and his shining pate with its ruff of wool whose silver hue implied a seniority attained only by the most hardened men, and above all with the air of stillness that trumpeted his murderous nature to all but the greenest travelers on this minor spur of the Silk Road, the African appeared neither to invite nor to promise to tolerate questions. Among the travelers at the caravansary there was a moment of admiration, therefore, for the bird's temerity when it seemed to declare, in its excellent Greek, that the African consumed his food in just the carrion-scarfing way one might expect of the bastard offspring of a bald-pated vulture and a Barbary ape.

For a moment after the insult was hurled, the African went on eating, without looking up from the shatranj board, indeed without seeming to have heard the remark at all. Then, before anyone quite understood that calumny so fine went beyond the powers even of the myna, and that the bird was innocent, this once, of slander, the African reached his left hand into his right buskin and, in a continuous gesture as fluid and unbroken as that by which a falconer looses his fatal darling into the sky, produced a shard of bright Arab steel, its crude hilt swaddled in strips of hide, and sent it hunting across the benches.

Neither the beardless stripling who was sitting just to the right of its victim, nor the one-eyed mahout who was the stripling's companion, would ever forget the dagger's keening as it stung the air. With the sound of a letter being sliced open by an impatient hand, it tore through the crown of the wide-brimmed black hat worn by the victim, a fair-haired scarecrow from some fogbound land who had ridden in, that afternoon, on the Tiflis road. He was a slight, thin-shanked fellow, gloomy of countenance, white as tallow, his hair falling in two golden curtains on either side of his long face. There was a rattling twang like that of an arrow striking a tree. The hat flew off the scarecrow's head as if registering his surprise and stuck to a post of the daub wall behind him as he let loose an outlandish syllable in the rheumy jargon of his homeland.

In the fireplace a glowing castle of embers subsided to ash. The mahout heard the iron ticking of a kettle on the boil in the kitchen. The benches squeaked, and travelers spat in anticipation of a fight.

The Frankish scarecrow slipped out from under his impaled hat and unfolded himself one limb at a time, running his fingers along the parting in his yellow hair. He looked from the African to the hat and back. His cloak, trousers, hose and boots were all black, in sharp contrast with the pallor of his soft hands and the glints of golden whisker on his chin and cheeks, and if he was not a priest, then he must, thought the mahout, for whom a knowledge of men was a necessary corollary to an understanding of elephants, be a physician or an exegete of moldering texts. The Frank folded his arms over his bony chest and stood taking the African's measure along the rule of his bony nose. He wore an arch smile and held his head at an angle meant to signify a weary half-amusement like that which plagued a philosophical man when he contemplated this vain human show. But it was apparent to the old mahout even with his one eye that the scarecrow was furious over the injury to his hat. His funereal clothes were of

rich stuff, free of travel stains, suggesting that he maintained their appearance, and his own, with fierce deter-
mination.

The Frank reached two long fingers and a thumb
into the wound in his hat, grimaced and with difficulty
jerked out the dagger from the post. He turned the
freed hat in his hands, suppressing the urge to stroke it,
it seemed to the mahout, the way he himself would
stroke the stubbled croup of a beloved dam as she ex-
pired. With an air of incalculable gravity, as if confiding
the icon of a household god, the Frank passed the hat to
the stripling and carried the dagger across the room to
the African, who had long since returned to his bowl of
stew.

"I believe, sir," the Frank informed the African,
speaking again in good Byzantine Greek, "that you have
mislaid the implement required for the cleaning of
your hooves." The Frank jabbed the point of the dagger
down into the table beside the shatranj board, jostling
the pieces. "If I am mistaken as to the actual nature of
your lower extremities, I beg you to join me in the
courtyard of this house, at your leisure but preferably
soon, so that, with the pedagogical instrument of your
choice, you may educate me."

The Frank waited. The one-eyed mahout and the
stripling, wondering, waited. By the door to the inn

The Frank jabbed the point of the dagger down into the table
beside the shatranj board, jostling the pieces.

yard, where the ostler leaned, whispered odds were laid and taken, and the mahout heard the clink of coins and the squeak of a chalk wielded by the ostler, a Svan who disdained the distinction between turning a profit from seeing to the comfort of his guests and that of turning one from watching them die.

"I'm sorry to report," the African said, rising to his feet, his head brushing the beams of the sloping roof, speaking in the lilting, bastardized Greek used among the mercenary legions of the emperor at Constantinople, "that my hearing shares in the general decay of the broken-down black-assed old wreck you see before you."

The African yanked the shard of Arab steel from the table and with it went in search of the Frank's voice box, ending his quest no farther from the pale knuckle of the Frank's throat than the width of the blade itself. The Frank fell back, bumping into a pair of Armenian wool factors at whom he glared as if it were some clumsiness of theirs and not his cowardly instinct for self-preservation that had cost him his footing.

"But I take your gist," the African said, returning the dagger to his boot. On the ostler's slate the odds began to run heavily against the Frank.

The African restored the shatranj board and pieces to a leather pouch, wiped his lips and then pushed past the Frank, past the craning heads along the benches and went out into the inn yard to kill or be killed by his insulter. As the men trooped after him into the torch-lit courtyard, carrying cups of wine, wiping their bearded chins on their forearms, the weapons belonging to the combatants were fetched from a rack in the stable.

If because of his immensity, the span of his arms and his homicidal air, and despite his protestations of senescence, which were universally regarded as gamesmanship, the betting had been inclined to favor the African before the weapons were fetched, the arming of the two men decided it. The Frank carried only a long, absurdly thin bodkin that might serve, in a pinch, to roast a couple of birds over an open fire, if they were not too plump. The travelers had a good laugh at "the tailor with his needle" and then pondered the mystery of the African's choice of sidearm, a huge Viking ax, its haft an orgy of interpenetrating runes, the quarter-moon of its blade glowing cold, as with satisfied recollection of all the heads it had ever lopped from spouting necks.

Under the full moon of the month of Mehr, with the torches hissing, the African and the Frank circled an ambit of packed earth. The Frank minced and scissored on his walking-stick legs, the tip of his bodkin indicating the heart of the African, glancing from time to time at his own fine black boots as they threaded a course through the archipelago of camel and horse turds. The African employed an odd crabwise scuttling style of circling, knees bent, eyes fixed on the Frank, the ax held loosely in his left fist. The awkward, almost fond way they went about readying themselves to murder each other moved the old mahout, who had trained a thousand war elephants to kill and so recognized the professional quality of the interest these two combatants were taking in the fight. But the other travelers jostling under the eaves and archways of the inn yard, who knew nothing of the intimacy of slaughter, grew impatient. They jeered the combatants, urging them to hurry so they could all finish their suppers and file off to bed. Half-maddened by boredom, they doubled their wagers. Word of the duel had reached the village down the hill, and the gate of the inn yard was lively with women, children and sad-faced lean men with heroic moustaches. Boys climbed to the roof of the inn, shook their fists and hooted as the Frank and the African emptied their heads of last regrets.

Then the ax, humming, seemed to drag the African toward the belly of the Frank. Its blade caught the torchlight and scrawled an arcing rune of fire in the gloom. The Frankish scarecrow dodged, and watched, and ducked when the ax came looking for his head. He dropped to his shoulder, rolled on the ground, surprisingly adroit for a scatter-limbed scarecrow, and popped up behind the African, kicking him in the buttocks with a look on his face of such childish solemnity that the spectators again burst into laughter.

It was a contest of stamina against agility, and those who had their money on the former began with confidence in the favorite and his big Varangian ax, but the African, angered, grew gross and undiscerning in his ax-play. He shattered a huge clay jar full of rainwater, soaking a dozen outraged travelers. He splintered the wheel spokes of a hay wagon, and as the solemn Frank danced, rolled and thrust with his slender bodkin, the berserker ax bit flagstones, shedding handfuls of sparks.

The torches guttered, and the tinge of blood drained from the moon as it rose into the night sky. A boy watching the fracas from the roof leaned too far out, tumbled and broke his arm. Wine was fetched, mixed with clean water from the well and handed in bowls to the duelists, who staggered and reeled around the inn yard now, bleeding from a dozen cuts.

Then tossing aside the wine bowls, they faced each other. The watchful mahout caught a flicker in the giant African's eyes that was not torchlight. Once more the ax dragged the African like a charger trailing a dead cavalryman by the heel. The Frank tottered backward, and then as the African heaved past he drove the square toe of his left boot into the African's groin. All the men in the inn yard squirmed in half-willing sympathy as the African collapsed in silence onto his stomach. The Frank slid his preposterous sword into the African's side and yanked it out again. After thrashing for a few instants, the African lay still, as his dark—though not, someone determined, black—blood muddied the ground.

The ostler signaled to a pair of grooms, and with difficulty they dragged the dead giant out to a disused stable beyond the present walls of the caravansary and threw an old camel skin over him.

The Frank straightened his cuffs and hose and re-entered the caravansary, declining to accept the congratulations or good-natured japery of the losing bettors. He declined to take a drink too, and indeed melancholy seemed to overcome him in the wake of the fight, or perhaps his natural inclinations toward Northern gloom merely resumed their reign over his heart and face. He chewed his stew and took his leave. He wandered down to the stream behind the caravansary to wash his hands and face, then slipped into the derelict stable, doffing his ruined hat as if in tribute to the bravery of his opponent.

"How much?" he said as he entered the stable.

"Seventy," the giant African replied, stringing the laces of his felt bambakion, its counterfeit bloodstains washed away in a horse trough, to the horn of his saddle. He rode a red-spotted Parthian, tall and thick-muscled, whose name was Porphyrogene. "Enough for a dozen fine new black hats for you when we get to Rhages."

"Don't even say the word 'hat,' I beg you," the Frank said, gazing down at the hole in the high crown. "It saddens me."

"Admit it was a fine throw."

"Not half so fine as this hat," the Frank said. He laid the hat aside and opened his shirt, revealing a bright laceration that ran, beaded with waxy drips of blood, across his abdomen. Flows of blood swagged his hollow belly. He looked away and gritted his teeth as the African dabbed at him with a rag, then applied a thick black paste taken from a pot that the Frank carried in his saddlebags. "I loved that hat almost as much as I love Hillel."

At that moment the animal in question, a woolly stallion with a Roman nose and its neck a rampant arch, stubby-legged and broad in the croup, the product of some unsupervised tryst between an Arabian and a wild tarpan, gave a warning snort, and there was a scrape of leather sole against straw.

The Frank and the living African turned to the door. Expecting the ostler, thought the old elephant trainer, with their share of the take, which included four of the mahout's own hard-won dirhams.

"You mendacious sons of bitches," the mahout said admiringly, reaching for the hilt of his sword.

CHAPTER TWO
────────

On Payment—
and Trouble,
Its Inevitable Gratuity

Easily as a sailor handling a blasphemy, the African reached behind him for the Viking ax (whose name, cut in runes along its ashwood haft, translated roughly as "Defiler of Your Mother"), but three little words preserved the cordial relations between the head and neck of the intruder, a wiry old party armed with a short sword, Persian by the look of him, with a knob of scar tissue where his right eye had been and a curious sneer. Many times the Frank, whose name was Zelikman, had seen his partner swing Mother-Defiler in order to silence, with a dull smack of meat and bone, some foolish shrewd fellow who had guessed the true nature of the duels that ill fortune sometimes obliged the partners to stage. Perhaps the span of a breath re-

mained to the intruder for the enjoyment of his perspi-
cacity, a breath that the Persian wisely employed to say:
"Keep your money." He returned his short sword to its
sheath, lifted a three-fingered hand from the hilt and
raised it, with its four-fingered mate, into the air. On
his right hip he wore an ornate weapon or tool, a carved
shaft of ivory barbed with a curious double blade like
a spearhead giving birth to a pruning hook. "I don't
want it, friends. No gold was ever harder won. As far as
anyone in this neighborhood will ever hear from me,
Nubian," the man continued, addressing his remarks to
Mother-Defiler rather than to Amram, who came in
fact from Abyssinia, "you are lying cold and lifeless
under a camel-skin blanket, and I am conversing with
your shade."

Amram winced, and his lips moved a little in recita-
tion of some Abyssinian charm intended to prevent the
misfortune that had been named from coming into the
world. Amram called himself a Jew, a son from the line
of the Queen of Sheba when she lay, amid the hides of
ibexes and leopards, with Solomon, David's son, but
as far as Zelikman had ever been able to ascertain,
Amram's only gods were those of fat luck and starveling
misfortune. Nonetheless he entertained superstitions
about ghosts and corpses, and only the profitability of
the bogus duels persuaded him to risk attracting the re-

gard of Death to the unusually protracted span of his life. The lean old Persian's little joke made Amram nervous, as did the prospect to Zelikman, for that matter, of being haunted by the giant black shade of his partner.

"What do you want, then, old cyclops?" Zelikman said, closing his shirt over the wound he had suffered, in the name of verisimilitude, during the fight. It stung painfully from the action of the ointment, a compound of wine, honey, barley mold and myrrh that Zelikman had been taught to formulate by his uncle Elkhanan, who in addition to being a rabbi and a great sage of the city of Regensburg had once served as physician to the court of Milan. The wound was not deep, but the specter of putrefaction terrified Zelikman in a way that the God of his fathers, despite strenuous efforts, had never quite managed to, and so he braved his pious uncle's ointment, though it made him irritable. "I don't like the sneer on your face."

"I am not sneering, I swear to you," the Persian said. "The errant tusk that spoilt my eye also cut the muscles of my cheek. I found myself endowed when it healed with this semblance of a contemptuous grin." The disfigurement of his cheek grew more acute. "Though it serves for most occasions when I quit the company of elephants."

"I have some training as a surgeon," Zelikman said, drawing Lancet, the slender blade that had excited such amusement among the travelers at the caravansary, and sketching out possible lines and angles of incision a quarter-inch from the mahout's good cheek. Lancet was a queerer instrument than even the other man's elephant hook, Zelikman supposed, edgeless and sharp at its tip, stiff but balanced in the hand, useless for any martial purpose but the judicious skewering of organs. It had been forged to order by the same maker of instruments who supplied the rabbi-physicians of Zelikman's family with their scalpels and bloodletting fleams, in sly defiance of Frankish law, which forbade Jews to bear arms even in self-defense, even when an armed gang of ruffians dragged your mother and sister screaming from their kitchen and did rank violence to them in the street while you, a boy, were obliged to stand bladeless by. Violence, circumstance, the recklessness of the apostate and a chance meeting with an African soldier of fortune had driven Zelikman to hire himself out as a killer of men, and Amram had taught him to take pains with the work, but Zelikman was a healer by nature and heritage, and though it had begun as a black jest, he now prized Lancet most for the mercy of its accurate thrusts. "Perhaps I should trim the other side to match. Give you a smile that better reflects your contentment with the wonders of this world."

Now it was the old mahout's turn to let a little joke make him nervous. He took a step away from Zelikman.

"You saw the young one I travel with?" he said. "Filaq, come out. I call him Filaq, in Persian that's—"

"Little elephant," Amram said. He was nearly as gifted at languages as the contumelious myna.

"Yes. You don't see it now, looking at this mess of bones, but the name suited him perfectly when he was young."

From behind a mound of fresh hay stepped the stripling to whom Zelikman had consigned his hat just before the fight. Sullen-shouldered, thin at the wrists, freckled and green-eyed, wrapped in a bearskin too warm for the evening and too fine for a dusty caravansary stinking of pack animals and cheeses, the stripling had as yet no shadow on his chin or lip, but he stood nearly as tall as Zelikman, and from the rosiness of his complexion, the gloss of his close-cropped russet hair and a commingled look of shame and haughtiness in his eyes, the physician from Regensburg was able to infer fifteen or sixteen years of good food, clean linens and the expectation of having his wishes granted. In the gloom of night that had filled Zelikman's soul upon the destruction of his hat, which had cost him thirty ducats in the market at Ravenna, the hand of fortune lighted a slim taper. The stripling in the bearskin gave off an aroma, more powerful than that of horse dung or cheese or one-eyed Persians, of money.

"Here is one whose safe delivery will pay better, I'll warrant, than your theatricals," the mahout said.

"We don't stoop to ransom," Amram said, no physician but a student all the same of men's corruptions. "Or truck with those that do so stoop."

"But I have not stolen him."

"And yet one sees at a glance," Amram said, signaling to Zelikman by means of a slight inclination of his silver-tinged head that it was time to get Hillel saddled and be on their way to the clearing, half a league beyond the village, where they had arranged with the ostler to take payment for their show, "that he is not here willingly."

"Indeed he is not," the mahout said in a tone of great weariness. "As he never tires of making clear to me. Three times since we left Atil that one has given me the slip."

"Atil," Zelikman said, and the little guttering flame burned steadier and brighter. "He is a Khazar?"

At the word "Khazar," the stripling began to nod, slowly, and now hope flickered also in the peridot eyes

The stripling spoke a few words in a language that sounded like the speech of Turks and then astonished Zelikman by murmuring a dreamlike phrase in the holy tongue of the Jews. His barbaric accent rendered the words indecipherable, but they remained pregnant with longing, and in Zelikman they stirred a strong desire to see the fabled kingdom of wild red-haired Jews on the western shore of the Caspian Sea, the Jewish yurts and pinnacles of Khazaria.

"Is there really such a place," Zelikman asked the stripling, in the holy tongue, "where a Jew rules over other Jews as king?"

"What's that?" said the mahout sharply, alert to the stratagems and deceits of his young charge. "What is he saying?"

"We discuss the boy's suggestion that we kill you, cyclops, and conduct him back to Atil, where his family will reward us generously for his return," Zelikman said, though of all the words spoken in the holy tongue by the stripling he in fact had recognized only one: *home*.

"I'd say that is unlikely," said the old fighting man. "Not that he said such a thing, for he would say or do anything if it might mean a chance to fly home and seek a fool's revenge." He reached for the ivory handle of his ankus and turned to the stripling. "Fool!" he barked,

"He would say or do anything if it might mean a chance to
fly home and seek a fool's revenge."

sounding very much as if he were scolding a recalcitrant beast. "What can you do, weak and friendless?"

The stripling's cheeks reddened, and he glared at his guardian, whose fixed sneer seemed cruelly apt.

"No," the mahout said, "you two could expect no reward from that quarter, I think, seeing as how his parents and his uncles are murdered, his aunts and sisters sold into brothels and his brother to the benches of a Rus long ship. And this one to be sold or killed, too, if I can't deliver him before we're hunted down. We have a day on them, maybe less. Which brings me to you gentlemen. I am trying to convey this hotheaded fool to safety among his mother's people, in Azerbaijan, to install him in the walls of his grandfather's house, his mother's father being by reputation a hard customer. Watching your display tonight, I was able to discern not only the sham of it but the murderous art that fools the spectator into believing. I have 200 miles to ride and a manhunt to elude before I can fairly say I have discharged my duty, and I'd like very much to have you two along to help me do that."

And he named a sum then, equal to five times the salary of a dekarch in the army of Byzantium.

"What did his family do," Amram said slowly, watching the boy, "that anyone should want to hunt them all down?"

"His father," the mahout said, "was the bek, or war king, of the Khazars. And my master. I kept the royal war elephants, forty-nine pachyderms of Africa and Hind. Thirty years and more some of them were with me. I counted them my friends, I don't mind saying. As did this stripling. He grew up in the elephant pens, so to speak. As much as among the pomps and fripperies of the court."

And there was something gauche or uncanny about the young prince, which Zelikman had been inclined to put down to inbreeding but now took for the fruit of having been raised with elephants.

"This past spring," the mahout continued, his voice falling to a mournful rasp, "comes the pox, out of Persia, that kills or cripples all the great sad brutes. And as the bek had made a great fuss over his elephants (of which at present the emperor in Byzantium has only forty-seven, that's a fact), putting the likeness of an elephant on his own personal arms, and so forth, well, the deaths looked bad. A bad omen, you see. Some of those that were already intriguing against the bek took heart from this pox. A general, name of Buljan, he seizes his main chance and ambushes the poor old elephant-fancying fool on the Kiev road. Installs himself in the Qomr citadel straightaway. Since then, Buljan's gone very carefully about the business of removing anybody—

brothers, wives, sons—who might be harboring feelings of resentment over the whole business."

"I am sorry about your animals, my friend," Amram said, taking his horse by the reins and leading it to the door of the stable. "But we don't stoop to politics, either."

"A word, Amram," Zelikman said. "If I may."

They sent the Persian and the stripling out into the inn yard then, and as was their inveterate custom at a crossroads of fortune, bickered like a couple of Regensburg fishwives. At first they argued about whether or not they had time to argue, or if arguing would cost them their appointment with the ostler in the clearing, and then about whose fault it had been that they were never paid by the landlord of an inn outside Trebizond, and then Zelikman succeeded in returning the conversation to the subject of the elephant boy, and his grandfather's stronghold in Azerbaijan, and the easy money that delivering him thence represented, at which point they resumed an old, old argument over whose definition of "easy money" was the least commensurate with lived experience, and about who was afraid and whose courage had been more openly on display in the recent course of their partnership. Next they argued about the overall equity of that longstanding arrangement and who shouldered more of its burdens, which led inevitably to the question of the hat, and whether the demands of verisimilitude had required its assassination. Amram had just dredged up an ancient debacle at Tergeste when there was a soft moan from outside the stable, and then a sharp thud, like a muffled bell, that to Zelikman's ears had the unmistakable timbre of a skull hitting a wooden plank.

When they got outside they found the body of the unfortunate mahout, from whose throat a black-fletched arrow protruded. They got their heads down, scanning the roof line, but it was too dark to see anything. Zelikman heard breathing behind him and turned to find the stripling, behind a rain jar, face buried in his hands, weeping. Zelikman was alien to feelings of sympathy with young men in tears, having waked one morning, around the time of his fifteenth birthday, to find that by a mysterious process perhaps linked to his studies of human ailments and frailties as much as to the rape and murder of his mother and sister, his heart had turned to stone.

"Shut up," he told the stripling, whispering the phrase in Greek, Hebrew, Arabic, Slavonic and, for good measure, Frankish, adjuring him to muzzle his goddamned snout. "Or I'll put an arrow in you myself."

But there was no time to make good on his threat because the next moment a drunken traveler stumbled out of the main hall of the caravansary and spotted Amram crouching down behind the wheel of a cart.

"It's the Nubian!" the traveler said, after his shock subsided, summoning his companions from their pots.

"I don't know why we couldn't leave when I *said* we should leave," Amram said.

Then the men of the inn were on them, in a roaring alcoholic mass of fists and boots and curses that would have shamed the foulmouthed myna. A gang of Avars went for the shed where the weapons were checked. Zelikman stumbled to his feet and punched and shoved his way back into the stable. He drove out the horses and sent them plowing through the mass of angry travelers and leapt onto Hillel's back as Amram fought his way into his own saddle. With a mezair and a cut to the left and a pair of caprioles, Zelikman danced the horse through the tangle of men. Two quick strokes with Lancet freed the purse from the belt of the ostler. Then they galloped through the gates of the inn yard and out onto the road.

They plunged into the cover of the woods and crashed along through blades and bars of moonlight, and it was not until they joined the road again and turned southward toward Azerbaijan that Zelikman noticed the stripling riding behind Amram, clinging to the big man's waist and looking back at the moonlit road behind them and the ever more distant home to which it ran.

CHAPTER THREE

On the Burdens and Cruelties of the Road

Whatever their merits as companions, the Khazar elephants had apparently failed to teach good manners to Filaq, who began to curse his guardians as soon as they had put a mile between themselves and the caravansary and continued to do so for days afterward, in a gargling, double-reeded tongue that seemed to have been devised for no other purpose. Over the four nights of the journey into Azerbaijan, as they picked their way down serpentine tracks and through thundering gorges—avoiding the main road, traveling in darkness—the stripling paused his recitations only to eat, to doze in the saddle or wrapped in his bearskin in their fireless camps, and to make the two attempts at flight that at last necessitated his being bound and tied to the cantle.

The attempted escapes followed sullen requests to be permitted to void his bladder, an act the stripling refused to perform in proximity to his hosts, which Zelikman took for elephantine modesty and Amram for arrogance, suggesting that no doubt Prince Filaq shat gold and pissed date wine. After Filaq failed to return the second time and they were obliged to backtrack four leagues up the slope of a vine-tangled, wasp-ridden mountainside to retrieve him, the partners bound him, but still he refused to favor them with the sight and smell of his royal excretions, and so Amram was regularly obliged to lead the youth on a leather thong far into the underbrush and leave him tied to a tree for a reasonable period before retrieving him.

"I have arrived at a new diagnosis," Zelikman said, sitting in the shade of a bear-shaped outcrop of green granite, his damaged hat brought low over his eyes, puffing on a short Irish dudeen whose bowl he filled with a paste of hemp seed and honey. While Amram did not share the habit, he encouraged it, because the pipe inclined his partner toward a more charitable view of the imperfections that marred creation, for which the Jews of Abyssinia blamed a host of energetic demons but which Zelikman attributed to creation's having occurred without divine will or intention, like the snarl of wrack and shells in a tide pool, a heresy that would have shocked a man more troubled than Amram by piety and which, like all Zelikman's heresies, afforded its promulgator no comfort whatsoever. "The family of the Khazar bek arranged to make it *look* as if they had all been murdered by this Buljan fellow, as a way to rid themselves once and for all of that boy."

Amram nodded, crouched on top of the rock, listening for the hiss of Filaq's water against the hillside and looking down along the gray-green folds and gray-brown escarpments and granite ribs of the hillside to the valley where they would find the grandfather's fortress with its stout walls and its treasury laid open to the noble rescuers. He could see a thin vein of smoke. At the far side of the valley ran a last halfhearted scatter of foothills before the Caucasus gave out at the sea.

"Perhaps they arranged to have themselves actually murdered," Amram said. "Just to make sure."

Zelikman allowed that over the course of the past few days in Filaq's scabrous company, he had entertained suicidal thoughts of his own, at which Amram spoke a formula in the Ge'ez tongue effective at averting the evil eye, because Zelikman was prey to spells of black bile during which he would contemplate—and one bleak night in the city of Trebizond had ingested— the deadly tinctures that he carried in his saddlebags.

"Of course grief may have driven the boy mad," Zelikman continued in a dreamy tone, lowering the hat still farther as the smoke of his dudeen worked its charm. "To lose his mother and father. His crown and his palace. His elephants too. I suppose we ought to pity him."

"Fine idea," Amram said. "You go first."

There was no sound from up the hillside now. He craned his head and saw that Filaq was halfway to the ridgeline, scrabbling on his hands in the scattering gravel, hurrying toward the home that lay a hundred leagues north, and its ghosts. Amram let loose a polyglot string of curses that would have done honor to the old myna of the caravansary, jumped from the rock and started after Filaq with long strides of his hard-pumping legs. The sun beat down on his head, and he sweated, and thorns tore at his clothes, but he had been pursuing the spirit of his stolen daughter, Dinah, for nearly twenty years, in dreams and among the roads and kingdoms, and a loudmouthed Khazar could offer nothing in the way of a challenge to the hunter of a ghost girl.

"No," Filaq said in wretched Arabic as Amram

caught hold of the remains of the thong, which he had chewed through, and dragged him into the shade of a tall fir tree. "Please, lord. To home, please, you take me."

He fell to his knees, and his large eyes, dazzling as the green armor of a scarab, filled with tears, and he employed with pitiable energy the tiny store that was known to him of Arabic's rich supply of blandishments and entreaties, insisting in broken phrases that he would rather be tortured and killed in Atil having at least made the attempt to avenge himself on Buljan than to live out his days as the ward of his grandfather's charity.

Amram looked away, confused by this unprecedented display of deference from one who had been employed, just an hour before, in calling down leprous growths and pustules upon him. He pulled Filaq to his feet, recalling like a man reviewing the history of his amours the days of his distant youth when he had sought and sometimes gained revenge. Then he retied the thong that had been chewed, braiding three pieces together this time to make a stouter cord, and dragged Filaq back down through the brambles to the rock in whose lengthening shadow Zelikman still lay, pondering one of the useless paradoxes or baubles of philoso-

"Please, lord. To home, please, you take me."

phy with which he amused himself when under the influence of his pipe. When he noticed Amram's return, he stood up and approached the stripling.

"Everything ends in death," he said in the holy tongue. "You know that, don't you?"

His expression was kind and his voice soft, teacherly. Filaq nodded.

"Therefore revenge is superfluous. Unnecessary effort. One day Buljan will be bones in the dust. And so will you and I and that behemoth holding your leash. Revenge is the sole property of God."

"I want him to suffer," Filaq said. "To hurt, to writhe in pain."

Zelikman blinked and then put his hand on Filaq's shoulder in a manner that showed both tenderness and scorn.

"You and God have a great deal in common," he said. "Now, will you ride calmly behind me or do we need to bind you at the ankles, too?"

Filaq seemed to consider the question very seriously.

"You had better bind my ankles," he said.

It was done, and then Zelikman hoisted Filaq and slung him across the withers of his horse. The stripling muttered for a while and somewhat belatedly wished tumors onto the testicles of Zelikman's grandfather, but as they drew nearer to the fortress, he curled up still and silent and seemed resigned at last to his fortune.

They were two miles upslope of the fortress when they realized the smoke was too thick and dense for a rubbish or cook fire. It boiled and poured into the sky. They tied the horses in a thicket along the bed of a stream in which a thin cold trickle of water ran and then crept along the stream bed until they were within half a league of the stronghold. Zelikman took from its pouch the curious glass that was his only patrimony, a pair of flattened clear beads, devised by some genius of Persia, mounted on brass wire one behind another in a way that made it possible to see distant things in detail. The partners passed the Persian glass back and forth, taking turns surveying the stronghold, a large house of timber, mud and tile set atop a conical hill whose base was encircled by stout walls. It burned zealously, sending up rolling shafts of black smoke veined at their root with fire and moaning like the mouth of a cave. The massive wooden gates hung splintered, poleaxed and smoking, and the ramparts were garlanded with the bodies of helmeted guards, slain attackers armored in Turk style and bareheaded household retainers who had gone to their deaths armed with kitchen knives and hayforks. Over everything hung an odor of burning hay, timber and a sweet stench of crackling fat that mocked both conquerors and conquered with its reminder of their universal nature as meat for the kites and buzzards that had already begun to draw lazy naughts across the high blue sky.

They watched the stronghold burn from the safety of the stream bed until the carrion birds began to alight and strut like princes on the walls and then, tying the dazed stripling to the overhanging branch of a willow, crept up to the shattered oak jaws of the gate and scuttled inside, blades drawn.

Someone was singing. Amram heard sawed strings and a voice at once lilting and raspy—an old man or woman—and they followed the sound of it up a crooked lane to the top of the hill, squelching through mud that was an impasto of dirt and blood, past the fly-blown carcasses of women, children and defenders alike, some three dozen people in all, among them a crone and a babe in arms. Amram kept up a steady murmur of prayers for the souls of the butchered and his own in this grievous shambles. At the top of the hill in the archway of the main house, an eyeless old man sat on a bucket, scratching at a two-stringed gourd, warbling weird melismas on a madman's text.

"Fine fellows," Zelikman said, surveying the charred remains of a storehouse in which greasy pools of what had once been stacked bales of wool still bubbled and popped.

"And numerous. Either the mahout underestimated or this Buljan has increased the number of men pursuing our young friend. I see the trace of at least a dozen horses."

They wasted an hour poking through the rooms and structures that had escaped the fire or cooled enough to permit inspection. But the storehouses and larders were all ash, and if the household treasury had escaped the looting hands of the attackers, it had not escaped the flames. In the end they returned to the stream bed empty-handed but for a pair of goats, handsome if singed. As they drew nearer to the willow tree where they had tied up Filaq, they found themselves confronted, and Amram confronted Zelikman, with the question of what to do, now, with their charge.

"There is no reason, at this point, not to consider him our property by right," Zelikman argued. "A gentleman of the road worthy of the title would convey him to the nearest slave market and see what price he fetched."

"I fear that explains our overall lack of success at this game, Zelikman," Amram said. "Because I'm not going to do that."

"No," Zelikman said sadly. "Neither am I."

But when they returned to the willow tree, they found no stripling, only the raveled strands of a camel-hide lanyard swaying like willow branches in the breeze. This discovery dismayed Amram, but he was inclined, according to the tenets of his personal philosophy, to accept it and go along their way. He might have persuaded Zelikman of the wisdom of this course, but when they went to find the horses they had tied up in the copse, they found their saddlebags and Porphyrogene but no trace of the gold from the inn or of the curly coated, big-nosed half-Arabian, Hillel.

Hastily they tied the goats, slung them from Porphyrogene's saddle and set off, riding tandem, up the track. Burdened by two riders, even a strong Parthian stallion could not hope to match the speed of the lithe and sure-footed Hillel, and by the time they reached the pass and the main road that descended in lazy switchbacks to the shore of the Caspian and then north to the city of Atil, Filaq's relative inexperience and unbalanced mental state held their only hope of retrieving him and, more important, Zelikman's horse, a loss that was already threatening to plunge Zelikman, the effects of his hemp pipe having long since dwindled, into a gloom that promised to be dark indeed.

"This accursed country into which you led us has already cost me my hat," Zelikman said. "Not to mention a sack of gold. But if it costs me Hillel too, I'll take it very ill indeed."

Amram refrained from pointing out, though not without effort, that this Caucasian jaunt had originated in a pipe dream of Zelikman's. He had already seen the broken turf up ahead and the shaft of a black-fletched arrow protruding from a blasted trunk at the edge of a clearing about forty feet farther along. He swung down from the horse and crouched, creeping along on his heels, reading the alphabet of horseshoe prints and other stray marks of struggle.

"Buljan's hunters have found him," he said presently, having concluded his study of the text in the dirt. "They caught him there. He struggled. He knocked one of them down. And then they tied him, here, and put him on a horse. And set off again. Headed north."

"Why didn't they kill him?" Zelikman said. "At long last?"

"Perhaps they did. But I see no sign of it."

"And Hillel? Yes. I see his marks."

He sat down under the blasted tree, and Amram could see him sinking, as a man watches the sun sink into the western sea, into the darkness of his thoughts. As little chance as they had stood of catching Hillel, their situation was now more hopeless still, for even if they somehow managed to catch the party of man-hunters, they would find themselves faced with odds of at least a dozen to one.

"Get up," Amram said.

Zelikman looked up at him, his face blank, soot-streaked, filling with that unshakable weariness as rapidly as a staved-in hull fills with cold black sea.

"Where is the point?" Zelikman said.

"Here," Amram said, drawing his dagger and holding it, as he had lately held it in the caravansary, less than the breadth of a finger from Zelikman's throat. "I would rather have your death on my conscience or, failing that, face a week's hard riding and a gang of armed bravos than suffer through a month or more of listening to your maunderings."

Zelikman considered the dagger and his partner's face and appeared seriously to weigh the three possibilities that Amram had just named. Then he held out his hand, and Amram dragged him to his feet.

"Just when did you acquire a conscience?" Zelikman said.

"A figure of speech. Which will it be?"

Zelikman yanked the arrow out of the charred trunk and handed it with a shrug to Amram.

"Only because I know how Hillel pines for me," he said.

CHAPTER FOUR

ON THE SUBSTITUTION OF ONE ANGEL, AND ONE CAUSE, FOR ANOTHER

All that remained of the temple, reared by Alexander during his failed conquest of Caucasia and affiant now to that failure and to the ruin of his gods, was a wind-worn pedestal and the candle stub of a fluted column, against which a would-be ruffian named Hanukkah sat propped with his right hand over the wound in his sizable belly, as he had sat for two long days and nights, waiting with mounting impatience for the angel of death.

He had failed as a farmer, a dealer in hides, a soldier, and now as a hunter of men, a trade he undertook on a misguided whim, riding as last-minute replacement for a more qualified killer whose career of violence ended in a tavern on the night before the hunting party set out from Atil to track down the last free survivor of Bul-jan's coup.

The other five manhunters who like Hanukkah had remained true to the cause—or at any rate to the gold—of their employer lay scattered around the ruin like the tumbled fragments of a colonnade. Among them were two of their erstwhile comrades, who had been turned by the haughty manner and readier gold of their prisoner and the promise of more gold to come. Distilled by the sun of two days, their stench was wafted tenderly in the direction of Hanukkah's nose by the beating wings of buzzards, which had arrived within hours of the slaughter, in their black finery, to feast.

Beside him, nestled in the crook of his left arm, lay a skin in which remained a few swallows of clean water, which Hanukkah had been denying himself in the hour since dawn in the hope of hastening his demise. His belly wound had ceased to cause him much pain, which he took as a favorable sign that the angel had concluded whatever other business had been delaying him and was hastening even now to collect him. The recriminations that assailed Hanukkah through the first hours of his vigil were faded to a philosophical regret at the waste that attended all human ambition. It was only his vain desire to gain the money he needed to purchase the freedom of his beloved Sarah, a whore in a Sturgeon Street brothel, that had led him to offer his sword in the murderous service of Buljan. Hanukkah had no quarrel with the old bek, and in fact had been inclined to view him as an able leader, worthy of loyalty and tribute. He had been an unwilling participant in the raid on the stronghold in Azerbaijan, and in fact had spent the hour it endured cowering under a hay wagon at the back of a stable.

Though only a week earlier the idea would have struck him as heresy, as he lay waiting to become carrion he considered that plump and vivacious Sarah was perhaps unworthy of his suffering and death, when after all, she chewed with her mouth open and her wind, when she had been consuming too much milk, gave off an unsettling odor of brimstone.

But when he remarked the travelers, a giant African and a black-hatted scarecrow crowded onto the broad back of a massive spotted horse that looked to be on the verge of collapse, Hanukkah forgot his resolve and took a long warm swig from his water skin. The sight of living beings who were not, presumably, eaters of dead flesh awoke a fresh desire in Hanukkah, despite the wound to his belly, to prolong his existence just a little while longer, and perhaps to see his plump Sarah once more.

"Friends," he called in Arabic, his voice a raucous barking.

The African reined in the tottering horse with its flecked lips and wild eye, and the travelers dismounted, the African with a weary grace and no expression, the scarecrow with grimaces and a show of soreness in the underparts. The big man unsaddled the horse, peeled away the blanket and led the spotted stallion from the slaughtered men and scavenger birds to a blotch of patchy grass in the unpersuasive shade of a gnarled juniper. There was a thin trickle of fresh water a few rods beyond the tree, and the horse lay down its ears and snorted, once, scenting it. The African patted the horse's neck and spoke to it in a velvet language, and Hanukkah caught sight of the broad ax slung across the giant's back and began to regret his decision to call attention to himself, because kindness to horses was often accompanied in soldiers by an inclination, when it came to men, to brutality.

The behavior of the second man was even more troubling, because as the Frank hobbled over to the ruined column where Hanukkah lay with his hand keeping his life in his body, he neither avoided nor ignored the sight of the carnage all around him but appeared actively to study it, stopping now and then to crouch beside a body and examine its situation and the nature

"Friends," he called in Arabic, his voice a raucous barking.

of its wounds. At last he reached Hanukkah and regarded him with pale, almost colorless blue eyes that were shadowed by the wide brim of his black hat. Eyes as clear and cold as the doom they seemed inclined to pronounce on Hanukkah.

"Are you the angel of death?"

"Even worse, fatty," the pale stranger said. "I'm the angel of fools."

He held Hanukkah's right hand and tried to pull it from the sword wound. As cold as his gaze appeared, his touch and his manner had something reassuring about them, and Hanukkah made no effort to resist. But he had been clutching his belly for so long with such force that his elbow would not unbend, and his hand was cemented in place by congealed blood.

"Don't go anywhere," the Frank said, and though it seemed impossible in this hostile place that fortune had chosen as the site of Hanukkah's death, he seemed to intend it as the sort of joke whose purpose was not to amuse, for there was nothing very amusing about it, but rather to reassure by suggesting that there remained to Hanukkah life enough to spare a little of it in polite pretending.

"You're a physician," Hanukkah realized, and in answer the Frank stood up, went to the saddlebags where the giant had dropped them, brought out a large leather drawstring pouch and a roll of canvas tied with ribbon and carried them back among the dead men to his patient. He unrolled the canvas, revealing a number of small steel implements whose function Hanukkah preferred not to imagine, and then unknotted the leather thong of the pouch. In the meantime, the black giant had begun his own survey of the campground, where three nights earlier Hanukkah and his fellows had shared a roast goat and a looted cask of sharab, and some fool had made the mistake of removing the gag from the stripling's mouth to see if, plied with drink, he might say or do something amusing. The African paid heed not just to the corpses but also to the situation of trees, rock and roadway, the footprints in the dust, the position of the sun in the sky. Looking at him, Hanukkah could not imagine how a man could differ more from the pale, fair scarecrow, but when the African came to stand beside his partner his eyes held an identical certainty of knowing what little there was of interest to know about Hanukkah, a paltry fatal handful of facts.

"Open," the Frank said. He held out a small pipe, the color of old bone, its bowl filled with a nasty-looking brown mixture, and when Hanukkah parted his cracked lips, the Frank struck a flint to the bowl of the pipe and encouraged Hanukkah to draw the thick, honeyed smoke into his lungs. Hanukkah coughed, and then drew again, and it was not long before he was aware of being filled, in rippling drizzles, by a stream of amber honey poured through his mouth and neck into the bottle of his soul. The scarecrow took hold of his arm again and slipped it from his belly like the loosened string of a robe.

When Hanukkah came to himself he was seated, slumped, on the back of his own horse, with a burning sensation in his midsection and his arms around the waist of the man who had saved his life and who was now engaged in an argument, in an unknown language, with the African on his spotted Parthian. The sun had dipped behind the slope of the mountain along whose eastern skirt ran the road that led, hugging the southeast littoral of the Khazar Sea, from Azerbaijan to Atil. The air was crisp, the light wistful and the smell of the Frankish physician abominable, and Hanukkah knew that he was going to live.

"Thank you," he said, or tried to say, but his throat was raw and his lips half-sealed, and it did not emerge loud enough to interrupt the dispute between the African and the Frank. He said, in Arabic, "Thank you for finding my horse."

The African left off making whatever irritated point he had been trying to score against the Frank, turned his great head toward Hanukkah and said: "Have you any objection to this fellow's taking it as payment for saving your life? Provided that we agree to convey you to water, food and a road home before we part ways?"

It was a reasonable and acceptable proposal, but there was a querulous note in the African's voice that made Hanukkah leery of agreeing too quickly.

"I am not sure my life is so valuable," he said. "But if the terms are agreeable to the learned gentleman. . . ."

"I don't want your old hack," the Frank said, and the bones of his back stood out against the dusty black leather of his jerkin. "I want Hillel. And do not repeat, Amram, that a horse is a horse, because history, circumstances and I have disproved that argument many times."

"The manhunters are two days ahead of us," the African said. "They're heavily armed and bound for a kingdom in which we have no business, no friends. Apart from your freakish half-Arabian sweetheart, for whom you have now, thanks to the openhandedness of this good Khazar, found adequate replacement, I see nothing that we stand to gain from the pursuit of that boy."

"Our money," the Frank said. "He has that too."

"I'm afraid not," Hanukkah said. "It was divided

among the bastards who put me and the others to the sword, with the promise of more on the boy's safe return to Atil, and greater reward still on the restoration of his family to the bek's tripod. He has an older brother named Alp, who was sold by the usurper into slavery among the Rus and whose cause the stripling advanced, along with the contents of his, or rather of your, sack of gold."

"The king of the great land of the Khazars rules with his ass slung in a tripod?"

"The bek is not our king," Hanukkah said, trying to explain how alone among the civilized peoples of the earth the Khazars, in their wisdom, had discovered a means by which men might, profitably and without excessive peril to their souls, serve two masters. There was the bek, who directed the daily course of men's affairs, in the teeming streets of Atil, in the profane worlds of warfare and commerce, and over him—over all the Khazar people, embodying them and their interests and speaking on their behalf to God and all his angels—there was the kagan, in his palace on his sacred island in the middle of the river Atil, whose word was law and whose face was never seen.

"A kagan is the father, the mother and the lover of all his people. Nobody would lift a hand against him," Hanukkah said. "But a bek has many enemies, and Buljan more than the usual. These enemies may have already begun to look for someone to oppose Buljan. I imagine that the boy, Filaq, could easily find men to finance the ransom of Alp. After that it would be a matter of mustering soldiers, and I can tell you, for I've seen it with my own eyes, that this youth has a way with soldiers. He talked two-thirds of our number into betraying both our employer and the other third, among which, alas, I found myself."

"Because you so love the cause of Buljan?"

"No," Hanukkah said. "I—I suppose it's only that I don't like changes in plan. I am slow to make up my mind."

"Slow-witted."

"If you like. But I obeyed an impulse in deciding to come along on this damned journey, and you see how that worked out."

The Frank turned on his horse now and stared at Hanukkah for a long moment as they started up the last rise before the pass. When they crested it, they would see the first shimmer of the Khazar, or Caspian, Sea, whose chill waters were no colder than the eyes of the Frank as they made their diagnosis of Hanukkah's heart.

"You did it for the sake of a woman, I suppose?" the Frank said.

"For Sarah," Hanukkah said. And he told them about the slave girl for the purchase of whose freedom he had enlisted in the deadly service of Buljan. "I'd never heard of this Filaq, to be honest, before I took this damned job. Never paid the slightest attention to royal genealogies or politics. Doubtless there is more to this story than I will ever—"

As they came around a bend in the road, Hanukkah's old nag shied, and reared up, and danced sideways into a thicket before the Frank succeeded in bringing it around, and then they sat a moment, staring at the dead men who had been laid by the side of the road in a neat row like the physician's instruments in his canvas roll. Kisa, Suleiman, Hoopoe, Bugha, they were all there, all nine of them, stripped of their weapons and armor, their waxen faces gawping at the sky. There was no sign of Filaq, or of the bag of gold.

They climbed down from their horses, and the giant unshouldered his ax. On one side of the road there was a sheer rock face and on the other a long, gentle rise to the pass. The rise was brown and treeless and could be concealing no one. They waited until it was dusk, and then as the bats began to circle they led the horses almost to the top of the rise, where they tied the animals and crept along on foot until they could see over the crest. Below them, widening like a horn, stretched a steep-sided valley that ran, in terraced ripples that were crosshatched with vineyards, all the way to the sea far below. About halfway down the slope, a great number of horses milled, cropping the grass. Beyond them, to the right of the road, Hanukkah made out the white tents, peaked and striped with green, of a company of Arsiyah, elite mercenaries, Muslims whose fathers had come from Persia two centuries ago and who had served the kings of Khazaria since long before the conversion of their employers to the teachings of the Jews. Hanukkah heard laughter, and the jangle of a lute, and smelled scorched grain and roast onions.

"Well, it looks like our boy found himself an army," the African said, shaking his head. "So much the worse for him."

CHAPTER FIVE

On the Observance of the Fourth Commandment Among Horse Thieves

With nightfall, a wind blew in over the sea, from the lands beyond the Khazar Sea and beyond the vast steppe of the north, from kingdoms of forest and snow that Amram understood to be the habitations of witches and snow djinn and warrior women who rode on the backs of bears and of giant deer. In the wind was a promise only of ice, storm and advancing darkness, and Amram knelt on the northern slope of a strange mountain, far from home, drew his woolen cloak more tightly around his shoulders and knew in his heart that he would end his days in some winter kingdom, among wintry men. Then, as if overhearing and taking pity on the maudlin trend of his thoughts, the wind carried to his nostrils from the fires of the troops camped in the valley the desert tang of a camel-dung fire, and with it the plangent cry of a soldier-muezzin calling his saddle-weary brothers to a belated Jumuah. Amram was surprised to learn that it was a Friday. Bearing this strangely moving information, he crept back down to the fold of rock in which Zelikman and Hanukkah had hidden themselves, and then led by Zelikman, who honored the commandments in nearly the same measure as he despised them, the son of Ham, the son of Shem and the son of Japheth bowed their heads to greet the Sabbath bride before they rode down the mountain, toward the winter and the sea, to steal back Zelikman's horse.

It so happened that soon after he first set out from his village in pursuit of his stolen daughter, Amram had been employed as a horse thief. It was a trade that he had continued to pursue intermittently ever since, in particular during his ten years of service in the armies of Constantinople, when he had been obliged, through the improvidence and cheeseparing of the emperor's quartermasters and longstanding custom of his border troops, to steal not only horses but also cattle, sheep, goats, fowl, grain, cheeses, fuel, skins, wool and hides. Everything but women: that was one custom Amram had always declined, while he held a command, to observe or to tolerate in his own men.

Amram supposed that Hillel must by now be accustomed to being stolen, having originally been provided to Zelikman during a raid the partners staged on a khan outside Damascus whose landlord, himself a broker of stolen horses, tried to cheat them after one of their performances.

After prayer they dined on the lees of their provisions and the last gristly hunks of goat, and Hanukkah offered thanks to God on their behalf, employing a Khazari melody that sounded throaty and sad to Amram's ear. Amram took out his shatranj board and thrashed Zelikman and Hanukkah twice apiece while they waited for the perfection of darkness. Then they crept back up to the crest of the pass.

Zelikman had tried to dissuade Hanukkah from joining them, in consideration of his wound, but Hanukkah would not hear of it, insisting that he felt so grateful to Zelikman for sewing him up so tightly, and salving him so efficaciously, that he was prepared if need be to crawl on his belly to the Arsiyah camp, and if tonight they should prove unsuccessful in retrieving the virtuous Hillel, then Zelikman might, should he ever choose to return home, ride on Hanukkah's back all the way to Francia or Saxony or the evening couches of the Sun himself.

"Take care of what you say," Amram advised him.

"He healed me of a sword cut to the neck five years ago, and I've been carrying him on my back ever since."

Then they started down in the darkness toward the horses. A hundred and ten, by Amram's count, strong animals well fed and stolid, they milled around the meadow to the east of the tents, a shifting patch of denser darkness against the night. Hobbled, loudly gourmandizing the dry chess grass, they were guarded by a pair of dismounted soldiers in long, dusty coats split up the front and elaborately bearing on the left sleeves embroidered quotations from the lips of the Prophet. A pair of pickets held the southern approach to the camp, and there were guards posted on the north and west sides of camp, all fine, tall, falcon-faced men, in excellent equipage and reasonable order, but to Amram's eye as he had studied them and their fellows in the last of the daylight they betrayed an indifference to their duty, a hint of discontent, as if they had better things to do and expected no trouble or enemy from any quarter. Something was roiling them. He wondered if perhaps they suffered from the discontent of indolence, patrolling a frontier that had been at peace too long, the last war between the Khazars and the armies of the Caliph having ended more than a hundred years ago. If they were men of spirit they might resent the posting and wish they could be in on the hot battles and fat prizes in the distant Crimea, where according to Hanukkah the armies of the new bek were busy reconquering the great cities of Feodosia and Doros to bring them under control once more of the candelabrum flag.

Dispatching the watchmen, discontented or not, was always the simplest part of a horse or cattle raid. In former times, Amram would have crept up on the pickets from their left and with one, two lateral strokes at the jugular sent them sinking to their knees. But it was true, as Zelikman argued, that if you were not swift enough in cutting their throats, men often managed to cry out, alerting their comrades, and sometimes you detached the head entirely from the neck, in which case there might sound, if you failed to catch it before it hit the dirt, a telltale drumbeat of the skull to give you away. Killing the guards could also lead to later reprisals. Amram saw the value therefore in letting Zelikman go to work in his own fashion.

They moved as slow through the deep darkness as blind men skirting a pit, groping their way from outcrop to outcrop, observing as well as they could the course that Amram had decided for them, a wide arc that ran twenty rods to the east before cutting back along a westward radius, approaching from the guards' left to gain half an instant on their sword arms if they managed to draw. Then as Hanukkah and Amram waited, backs pressed against a sheltering rock, Zelikman loped, hunched down, toward the pickets, who stood, about forty feet apart, with their backs turned to each other, arguing the merits of Barbary horses. The moon rose, and in her faint, cool light Amram and Hanukkah watched Zelikman creep along. In his long and skinny shanks there was none of the grace but all the intensity of a cat going about its fatal mousing, the patience, the grim reserve of a predator. He rose up behind the nearer picket, covered the man's face with his leather-gloved hand and embraced him with the other arm. A moment later he eased the man to the earth. When, rarely, Zelikman recalled his mother to Amram, it was often a bedside memory of her seeing him through fevers and nightmares, or singing to him in the soft Latin dialect of her grandmothers, and the shade of that unknown Jewess always seemed to appear in Zelikman when he anesthetized a guard or watchman and laid him tenderly on the ground. In his bag of salves and pastes, Zelikman kept a large packet, a leaf of papyrus wrapped around a cake compounded of henbane, mandragora and nightshade, which when dissolved in a special preparation of vitriol, decanted onto a bandage and applied to the nostrils and mouth could induce a profound and instantaneous sleep. Hanukkah watched from behind the rock with his eyes wide and admiring as Zelikman went to work on the second picket and laid him out beside the first.

As they cut across the grass, moving more quickly now, toward Zelikman and the horses, Amram could hear the snoring of the soldiers in their tents beyond. A last cricket scratched mournfully at its rebab. The stars wheeled toward winter, and there was light enough now to make out the blazes on the crops of some of the horses. Amram could smell the dusty musk of horsehide and the sour sugar on their breath. He pulled his bit of Arab steel from his boot and moved among the legs of the horses, cutting the thongs that hobbled them one by one. The animals began to question one another with a sense of urgency that Amram could feel increasing, passing rumor and confusion among themselves. It would not be long before their agitation grew loud enough to alert the other pickets or wake the men snoring in the nearest tents. Amram was counting on the agitation, relying on the horses as sowers of panic, but that panic must not be permitted to flower in the wrong garden. He stood up and tried to find Zelikman in the dark, muscular flow of dismay and alarm around him and caught sight of the long, disdainful face of Hillel, his droll eye, just as Zelikman found him and swung up onto his back.

Amram mounted the horse that was nearest him, its girth feverish between his knees. For a moment the shadows and the smell of dust overwhelmed him, and his horse would not move, but he spoke a few words to it in Ge'ez, the mother language of humanity according to his people, the sound of which always had a pacifying effect on horses. As he spoke to the horses around him, they began to follow his mount, Amram squeezing his knees together and telling the horse how beautiful it was and how much he loved it, and they gathered speed and the rest of the herd came after. He could hear the chuff of their breath and now cries from the tents, a shout of the picket on the other side of the camp. The stampeding horses opened up and stretched toward the tents and the guttering fires of the Arsiyah. The moment arrived at which, by his own longstanding custom and the needs of the situation, he should peel off and let the horses carry on through the camp to dispose as they saw fit of the tent strings and the soldiers and rejoin Zelikman on higher ground.

That was when the melancholy he had been carrying seemed to break him open, and the face of his lost daughter was confounded in his heart with the face of the young prince of the Khazars, who, having been apprehended by these soldiers, must eventually be conveyed by them to the usurper Buljan, their commander.

It was the business of the world, Amram knew, to manufacture and consume orphans, and in that work fa-
therly love was mere dross to be burned away. After
long years of blessed absence, the return of merciful
feelings toward what was, after all, only another motherless and fatherless child, struck Amram, bitterly, as a
sign of his own waning powers to live life as it must be
lived. Mercy was a failing, a state of error, and in the
case of children a terrible waste of time.

Amram steadied himself without stirrups or reins,
taking up a coarse fistful of mane, and lowered his
head. In an instant he was in among the shouting men,
the blazing brands, the screams of horses, tents collaps-
ing and flapping like bats into the sky. The folly of his
deviation became clear to him immediately. The moon
shed too little light. He would never find the boy in this
confusion.

He felt the great pumping heart—the fist of muscle,
bone and sweat between his knees—torque and shud-
der, and there was the crack of a joint. He flew forward
over the head of the horse, letting go of its stiff brush
of a mane, and the size of his frame carried him so
powerfully forward that he actually dragged the horse
down on top of him as he went. They rolled over, and as
if lightning and thunder had reversed themselves he
tasted blood in the back of his mouth, and the hammer

"Hear that sound, boy?" Amram said. "That's Zelikman."

blow of a hoof landed squarely on his chest. He had a vague impression of men's hands taking hold of him by the arms, hoisting him to his feet, and then after that he felt and heard nothing for what seemed like a very long time.

When he opened his eyes, his arms and legs were tied, and he heard horses shying and the whistling of a whiplash blade that he knew at once to be Zelikman's. He lay on the ground inside a musty tent against whose wall firelight flickered and distended shapes swelled and lapsed in the manner of a shadow theater. Filaq lay beside him, on his side, with his arms tied and a gag in his teeth. Amram's own mouth remained free.

"They got sick of listening to you too?" he said.

Filaq nodded.

"They hurt you?"

He shook his head.

"Do they know who you are?"

Filaq considered the question for a moment and began to give his head a shake before settling on an in-expressive shrug.

"Hear that sound, boy?" Amram said. "That's Ze-likman. Thinking he can rescue me. One skinny little Jew with a needle. Think he can do it?"

Filaq shook his head.

"Well, you're right. He was as big a fool to come

after me as I was to try to come after you. Should have just left you to your own sad devices."

The whistle and clang of Zelikman's sword stilled, and a captain cried out an order. Then silence. A moment later the flap of the tent was thrown open. Hanukkah came stumbling in, pitched forward as if shoved from behind, and fell sprawling on the ground. He lay there sobbing and heaving for a moment while Amram listened for news from the shadow show on the other side of the tent wall, so that he would not have to ask the Khazar if the friend of his life was dead.

CHAPTER SIX

ON SOME PECULIARITIES
IN THE TRADING PRACTICES
OF NORTHMEN

I t was remarked by one of the eminent physician-rabbis of the city of Regensburg, in his commentary on the Book of Samuel, a work now lost but quoted in the responsa of Rabbi Judah the Pious, that apart from Torah the only subject truly worthy of study is the science of saving men's lives. Measured by the criterion of this teaching—propounded by his grandfather—Zelikman counted two great scholars among his present acquaintance, and one of them was a horse.

As he backed, feinting and thrusting with Lancet at the Arsiyah who surrounded him, all of them wide awake now but not entirely free, as any of them would have been ready to attest, of dreamlike bafflement at the sight of a gaunt moonlit phantom who menaced them with an overgrown bloodletting fleam, feeling his way with the boot heel of his hind foot through the doubtful maze of unstrung tents and plunging horses that loomed at his back, Zelikman felt a sharp jab on the shoulder. He whirled to find that he had been bitten, with implicit reproof at his foolhardiness in trying to rescue Amram single-handedly from an entire company of heavily armed cavalrymen, by the bastard offspring of a mountain tarpan and an Arab dam whose bloodlines ran all the way back to one of Al Khamsa, the five mother mares of the Prophet's own stable.

Zelikman threw his arm around Hillel's neck and nodded to the soldiers, and murmuring a phrase in the horse-charming mother tongue of his Abyssinian partner urged Hillel to split the narrow gap between two huge men with lances who were just now bearing down on him. Then, displaying no grace whatsoever and suffering a painful encounter between his teeth and his tongue, Zelikman executed the difficult maneuver of mounting a horse at full gallop. To outside observers, of which thankfully there could be, in the darkness, on this desolate slope, very few, he must have looked as if he were trying not to mount Hillel's saddle so much as to perform some foul outrage upon his neck.

The grooms had been busy gathering in the scattered horses, and troopers were soon mounted and in pursuit of Hillel as he carried Zelikman back up the slope heading south. But while the Khazar horses, like Hillel, were sturdy and sure-footed and bred to the steep, rocky tracks, all heart and lung and back, with hooves so hard they required no shoes, they lacked speed and Hillel's ineffable Arabian humor: a demonic intelligence that lay somewhere between perversity and fire. By the time he gained the pass, the pursuers were far behind. Hillel chose his way down to the fold in the rock where Hanukkah's dray and Porphyrogene waited. Zelikman drew a slow breath that felt as if it might have been his first inhalation since the moment he had seen Amram charging bareback into the heart of the camp. As he breathed out, tears came to his eyes. He wept silently, after the custom of shamed and angry men, so that when the pursuit party came tumbling, pounding, scrabbling down the trail, past the fold in which he and Hillel stood concealed, he could hear the creak and rattle of their leather armor with its scales of horn; and when the Arsiyah returned, just before daybreak, at the very hour when all of creation seemed to fall silent as if fighting off tears, Zelikman could hear the rumbling of the men's bellies and the grit in their eyelids and the hollowness of failure sounding in their chests.

He waited until he saw a small lizard emerge from a fissure in the rock and creep toward a narrow medallion of sunlight on the granite. Then he led Hillel up over the rise again and back down into the valley, where the tents had been struck and the horses rounded up and saddled and the troops moved out north along the road. Zelikman followed the track northward for five leagues or more and then came to a barren place where another road branched away running northeast toward the shore of the Caspian sea. A small mound of stones marked the presence in this place, at one time if not today, of some ancient god of the crossroads. If you kept on to the north you would come, Hanukkah had told them, to Atil, the Khazar capital, at the mouth of a river that was also called Atil, though some called it Volga. A fresh trail of horse dung and hoof prints marked the northeast road; the Arsiyah were bound for the Caspian shore.

He followed them east for two days, in a steady downpour most of the way, through flooded gorges and spattering mud. The Arsiyah drove themselves hard, taking brief rest, lighting no fires, and after a day of bitter pursuit Zelikman understood the cause of their desperation: they were rushing to the relief of a regiment or a town that they feared might already be lost. Near dawn of the third day he caught his first whiff of the sea and narrowed the distance between himself and the Muhammadan troops until he could see the thongs of cloth-of-gold that enlaced their black queues, the splashes of mud on their leggings. As he came up a rise, he smelled smoke, and half a breath later he saw it, boiling and black. A thick, greasy smell like that which had hung over the stronghold in Azerbaijan. It was the smell of burning animals.

Hillel nickered and stepped sideways, and Zelikman mocked him tenderly for his cowardice. He swung down from the saddle and crept up to the top of the rise and trained the Persian glass on the ruination of a walled town built beside a broad estuary, flat roofs and minarets and a great white mosque giving up their matter and form to heaven in black gas and thick flakes of ash. Through the wooden gates, long strings of men and women and animals knotted and coiled as the townspeople abandoned their lives.

Along the waterfront, burned ships broke slowly into black pieces, and the slant sails of dhows caught fire. Standing off beyond the shallows, dragon prows surveyed the despoiling of the walled town. Fair-haired Northmen in jerseys of barbarous red poled out to their ships on wide barges heavy-laden with bales and casks, with kegs and sacks and huddled women, and handed them up to their fellows on the decks, and poled back to the wharves again for more. The red-shirted men swarmed in the streets, and a dozen of

Long strings of men and women and animals knotted and coiled as the townspeople abandoned their lives.

them were at work with irons, prying loose the golden sheeting that clad the domes and minaret spires of the great mosque. They worked quickly, and without their usual piling up of booty on the shore for the elaborate rites of their thievish creed, probably because some lookout not distracted by rape or robbery had chanced to gaze down from the shattered walls of the city and see the company of horsemen charging hard for the town gates.

There was a turbulence around those gates now as, driving out the survivors, bright-shirted men put their shoulders to the oak beams and sealed off the living from the dead, the loot from the looted, and bought themselves the time they would need, or so they hoped, to get away. Zelikman had observed firsthand the thievery of Northmen, whom the people of this shore called "the Rus," and what he had not witnessed he had learned from Amram, who had served alongside blond giants in the armies of the emperor. They were insane with bravery and fools for battle, but like men from one end of the world to the other, they were slaves to their appetites and to their love of treasure, and with their decks piled high with gold, fresh meat and casks of Georgian wine, the Northmen must as a matter of highest principle choose profitable retreat over the doubtful glories of combat.

As they rode to relieve the town, the advance riders of the Arsiyah became entangled, as the Rus had doubtless planned it, in skeins of fugitives with their bundles and their animals. In the time it took the advance guard, plunging and kicking and laying about them with the blunt ends of their lances, to clear a path, the remainder of the company caught up. Through the Persian eyeglass Zelikman could clearly make out, in the midst of the surging horsemen, Amram and the youth, mounted together, something stiff in Amram's carriage betraying to Zelikman's eye that his hands were probably bound, and beside them Hanukkah slouched on the back of a desert ass. There was a delay as orders were given and lamentations heard and prayers offered, and then half the company was divided in two and sent to flank the walls of the city and gain the river mouth, where even now a lone barge set out toward the long ships with the last great fistful of plunder, poled with wild discipline by a dozen red-shirted men. The remaining half of the black-armored Arsiyah dismounted to confront the barred gate. They could not know, as Zelikman saw plainly from the top of the rise, that the Rus had abandoned, or perhaps it would be more accurate to say they had perfected, their conquest of the city.

The troopers set about scaling the towers that

flanked the gate, but they could not gain a toehold in the masonry, and so they improvised a harness from rope and lashed a half-dozen horses together and set the team to work pulling at an iron hasp in the left-hand door. This proved to be futile as well, and men were sent to pile kindling at the doors' base. Then Amram leapt from the horse and held out his arms, and his bonds were cut. He took hold of the rope that still bound the horses to the gate and, with a slap on the hindquarters of the biggest animal, put his own back into the effort. Zelikman could hear the singing of the rope and the low oaken moaning of the gate, followed a moment later by an echoing bang like the crack of an immense whip. The doors fell open, and with ululating cheers the riders poured into the city they had arrived at too late to save. The last Northmen hauled themselves, along with their booty, onto the only ship that had not yet set sail just as the first Arsiyah rode out onto the burning wharfs. Under the weight of horses and armor the wharfs collapsed, throwing up a spectacular cloud of vapor and sparks.

Zelikman lowered the eyeglass, returned it to its doeskin pouch and then summoned Hillel and drove him at a gallop down to the town. The Arsiyah had seen him only by moonlight, with his hat lowered and his cloak flying. And if prior circumstance had inclined them to view him as an enemy—through soldierly habit, and because of his undeniable theft of the horse they had stolen from those who had stolen it from Zelikman, who had stolen it from a thief—the Arsiyah would now be in need of him, with his salves and his ointments and his willingness to stoop to the lowly work of the surgeon.

In the first group of refugees he fell among he found a dozen burned, punctured, battered and maimed, bleeding from raw and tumultuous wounds. Rumor of the miraculous advent of a white-skinned barber soon traveled all the way to the mouth of the river and back, so that to ride the seven rods that lay between him and the city gates required the remainder of the daylight, the better part of his pharmakon and his entire stock of fine silken thread.

He entered the city caked in blood, hungry and hollowed out, having vomited twice in the course of the day in reaction to the odors emitted by particularly vile wounds, his eyes stung by smoke, the wailing of babies haunting his ears. He sat his horse, hardly aware of the crackling fires, the barren doorsteps and the empty holes of housefronts, the carrion birds, the soldiers who gaped at him as he passed, trusting Hillel to search out and choose the street or alley that would lead to Amram. They passed into a narrow defile flanked by high houses that reached out for one another as they rose overhead until they were parted only by a cool dark band of twilight. The horse's shoeless hooves struck the paving stones with a knock like iron on bones, and then they emerged into a broad square, nearly as spacious as the piazza at Ravenna, and there on the wide steps of the despoiled mosque, one of whose minarets stood blackened and frail as a burned-out brand, with his arm around the slim shoulders of Filaq and a snoring Hanukkah curled at his feet, wearing the dice-playing smile of a man who could never be surprised, sat Amram.

He rose a little unsteady to his feet. His face was streaked with ash, ash lay on his hair and scalp and his eyes were crazed with pink. He came wincing down the steps of the mosque as if his back or hips were bothering him, and he and Zelikman fell into each other's arms. From within the mosque came the broken voices of men at prayer. Amram stank of burned tallow, smoke and a hard day's labor, but underneath it all there was the familiar smell of him like sun on dusty sandstone. The sound of prayer found some kind of grateful echo in Zelikman's heart.

"Late as usual," Amram said.

CHAPTER SEVEN

ON THE SEIZING
OF A LOW MOMENT

Hanukkah had been kicked awake by worse men, among them his own father, and so the curses he muttered, with his eyes shut and the honeyed hand of a dream still caressing his thigh, extended no further into history than the African's great-grandmother and confined themselves to envisioning her use by scabby Pecheneg stallions, making only glancing reference to the attentions of Bactrian camels. The true object of Hanukkah's spleen was wakefulness itself and the world that it would oblige his five outraged senses to certify. Hanukkah had soldiered in the army of an empire at peace and had thus dealt and witnessed death only in small batches, and he was shocked by the scale of slaughter he had seen today, wrought by foreign in-

vaders against Khazar men and women like him—
children of Kozar the son of Togarmah the son of
Gomer the son of Japheth the son of Noah—"people of
the felt walls," burners of dung fires, sworn to the solitary god of the clear blue sky, whether that god was
called Tengri, Jehovah or Allah. Most of all he was
shocked by the pointless butchering of a stranded Rus,
mute, dazed and trembling with some fever, white as a
fish belly, who was dragged by the Arsiyah from his hid-
ing place and slashed open like a gushing sack of wine.
After that, Hanukkah curled up on the steps of the
mosque and withdrew into sleep and his dream of
Sarah, of the faint smell of burning sandalwood when
she took his head into her lap, a dream from which
Amram's toe now dislodged him with all the tenderness of a boathook.

Hanukkah sat up, and opened his eyes, and saw
amid the smoke, dust devils and steady snow of ash a
gaunt, bloodied figure, tottering, asleep on his feet, his
black cloak crusted and dragging behind him, the air
around him wavering in a madness of flies.

At the sight of the Frank who had saved his life,
Hanukkah felt something swell inside him, like the
bladder that kept a sturgeon buoyant and swimming
true in the dark of the Khazar Sea. Men could be broken more terribly than he had ever imagined; but they

could also be repaired. Hope was a powerful cordial, and for a moment, with the burn of it at the back of Hanukkah's throat, he could only stand there, barking like a goose. Then he wiped his face on his filthy sleeve and hurried to Zelikman's side.

"Sit," he said, "please."

He sat the Frank down on the steps, pulled off his boots and fetched some water from a cistern. Some of the water he mixed with wine and passed to Zelikman in an overturned steel helmet. The rest he used to wash the blood from Zelikman's hands and face and to bathe his feet. From this mild and voluntary act of self-abasement, from the routine business of cistern and dipper and the wringing of a cloth, from the Frank's pale feet with their surprisingly soft ankles, Hanukkah derived a measure of comfort and regained his spirits. He found a neglected passage behind the mosque that the Rus had disdained to plunder, and in a cellar there a pair of toothless old sisters who at extortionate prices provided him with cold porridge, some lentils and mint, a bag of apples and the butt of a lamb sausage. He gave the food to Zelikman, who ate, and drank, and rested, talking to the African in Greek or Latin.

The subject of their conversation appeared to be Filaq, who sat slumped on the steps of the mosque with his chin in his hands, wearing a mask of tear streaks and

ash. The stripling had scarcely moved in the hours since
the Arsiyah mercenaries had paroled their prisoners to
shift for themselves, saying nothing at all for what
struck Hanukkah as an abnormally long period of time.
With his smudged cheeks and staring eyes he seemed
younger than ever, a child with an empty belly too
weary to sleep. He did not appear to notice when the
Arsiyah at last came trudging out of the mosque and
clattering down the steps around him, stooped as by
time or a heavy load, their gait uncertain, their evening
lifting of their voices toward far-off Mecca having done
little to ease the painful knowledge of their failure to
defend this Muhammadan town from destruction by
the Northmen. They loitered in the square, cast down,
aimless. Their commander was dead, drowned in the
collapse of the wharves. The surviving captains could
not come to agreement on whether they ought to pursue and punish the Rus or return to Atil and face con-
demnation, and possibly execution, by the bek for
having disobeyed his direct order that no one interfere
with or harass the Northmen in their "trading mission"
among the peoples of the littoral. This order was accompanied by rumors that these same ambitious
Northmen had backed the new bek in his coup; but an
order it remained. Now the Arsiyah, whose most
prized asset as with all mercenary elites was not their

skill at arms and horsemanship or fearsome reputation but the stainless banner of their loyalty, found themselves confronted by the dawning awareness that the only thing less forgivable than a mutiny was a mutiny that failed.

"They will go south, to Derbent," said the first captain, a florid, gaunt man bleeding from a dozen cuts, naming the next great Muslim town on the littoral. "We must anticipate them there."

His fellow captain, stout and languid of manner, pointed out the unlikeliness of their arriving at Derbent in time or force enough to stop the Northmen, who had the advantage of a prevailing north wind, and then by way of epilogue composed on the spot an unfavorable judgment on the gaunt captain's intelligence in even offering such a futile suggestion. The two officers were separated by their men only long enough to permit a general exchange of insults that soon devolved into a melee. In the course of the fighting, the lean captain ran onto the sword point of the stocky one and added his own life to the day's grim total and to the slick, rank slurry of blood and dust that filmed the square.

A shrill horseman's whistle split the air, and the soldiers abandoned the violence of their grief and turned to listen to the words of a trooper who had stayed out of the fracas, a wiry, bowlegged veteran nearly as grizzled as Amram, one of those men of no great rank or bravery who by virtue of heartlessness, opportunism and a long streak of luck outlasted all their fellows and so ranked as secret commanders of their troops. When this old veteran had the ears of his comrades, he explained, with patience and regret, and with Hanukkah keeping up a whispered translation into Arabic for the benefit of Amram and Zelikman, that they must now consider their company disbanded and, each man taking a share of water and food and a horse, scatter to the winds and the mountains, like drops of mercury on a rumpled carpet. In Hanukkah's view there was merit in this suggestion, but it was so greatly outweighed by shame and ignominy that a number of Arsiyah, unable to refute the old veteran's wisdom, sat down in the shadow of the mosque and cried.

The spectacle of weeping cavalrymen seemed to have a stimulating effect on Filaq. He rose to his feet, nose wrinkled as if in disgust, fists balled at his sides, and called for the men's attention. In his thin and reedy voice, he harangued the troopers in terms that made the most hardened soldiers among them flush, while those who had been lamenting fell silent. One or two sniggered at the youth's use of a particularly vile Bulgar epithet and smiled at each other under lowered brows.

"What does he say?" Zelikman asked Hanukkah.

"He says," Hanukkah said in a whisper, "that he has a proposition to make, but it is to be heard only by men in full possession of their manhood, and not by a mob of blubbering grandmothers who would spare the Northmen the trouble of gelding them by performing that service upon themselves."

"What proposition?"

"I can only imagine," Hanukkah said, "having sampled his wares in that line a week ago, sitting around the fire with my fellow gentlemen of the road."

But now that Filaq had the attention of the soldiers, he seemed to lose his nerve or his taste for handing out abuse, and wavered, blinking and swallowing, as if the thread of his own argument eluded him. Amram glanced at Hanukkah, then rubbing his chin contemplated the soldiery, who stood in the square gazing down at their bloody buskins like farmhands awaiting the lash. In one of their Western tongues Amram put a solemn question to Zelikman. Its import appeared to consist in assessing his partner's readiness for some hard business whose profit was outweighed by its impracticability. Zelikman's face expressed first grave reservation and then utter lack of interest. Amram went to Filaq and took up a place just behind and to the right of him.

"Go on," Amram told him, in passable Khazari, giving him a gentle push. "Do it."

Filaq pushed back, the expression on his face wondering and doubtful, reluctant and eager, returned for an instant to childishness.

"It isn't going to work," he said.

"Probably not," Amram agreed. "It's a terrible idea. But it seems that nobody here has a better one."

Filaq nodded and climbed to the top step of the mosque. He ran the back of a hand across his forehead and stood looking down at the weary soldiers, searching for the words to wake them.

"Do they know who he is?" Zelikman said. "Who his father was?"

"They will now," Hanukkah said.

So Filaq told his story, turning fine phrases in the dialect of the palaces and gardens. He asked them first to remember the fair and temperate rule of his father, the late bek, of whom, he now revealed, he was the youngest son. At this there was a murmuring among the soldiers, and one of them said that indeed Filaq resembled very strongly the late bekun, whom the soldier had seen once during the festivities attending the Feast of Tabernacles in Atil.

Next Filaq reminded them of the kindness and consideration that his late father had always shown his

At this there was a murmuring among the soldiers. . . .

Muslim subjects, and above all his faithful Arsiyah mercenaries, of whom he, Filaq, had heard it said and been ready to believe that they were the very last troops in the Army of Khazaria to swear loyalty to the usurper Buljan. The Arsiyah agreed that this could not be gainsaid, and a notion of the business the youth was about to propose began to blow among the enervated and downcast soldiers like a wind through dry rushes.

"We can be at the gates of Atil in two weeks," Filaq said. "Along the way we will surely pass through other towns, cities of the Prophet that have known defilement by the Rus. When they see your example, your loyalty to the family of my father, that great respecter of the property and the faiths of all his peoples, they will flock to our banner. By the time we reach the capital there will be thousands sworn to the cause of restoring the true heir: Alp, my good, my wise and pious brother, that strong fighter, that wolf of our ancestors, that keeper of the law common to Jews and Muslims, whom Buljan sold to the Northmen. Thousands! Ten thousand!"

"Hundreds, at least," the old veteran said. "Possibly even dozens."

The wind of righteous adventure that had begun to sweep through the square subsided as this secret captain and master of the accumulated lore of soldierly skepticism began to explain that any king who controlled both the treasury and the army was, in the eyes of the world, legitimate, and that while no one could know the mind of God, the Almighty had in the past shown a marked tendency, in his view, to ratify public opinion. If the Rus had treated the towns along the coast between here and Atil as harshly as they had this poor ruin, a rebellion could hope for little to feed them along the way, let alone to swell their ranks. He had just begun to describe the torments that, he understood, awaited those convicted of mutiny when, taxed apparently by lack of food and drink and the exhaustion of the past week, his eyes rolled in their sockets, and his head tipped backward, and he slid boneless to the ground, where, fortunately for him, his skull was spared fracture by the timely action of Zelikman, who caught him and eased him to the ground, concealing the pad of wadded chamois in his fist so adroitly that Hanukkah was certain no one saw it but him.

"God has silenced this man and his cowardly counsel," Amram said in Arabic, the mother tongue of the Arsiyah. "Perhaps you would do well to heed this indication of His will."

There was general acclaim at this suggestion,

shouts and whoops and wild ululation of the steppes, but it all ceased abruptly when Filaq pumped his fist and cried: "Alp! Alp!"

There followed a silence broken only by the wind hissing in burned rafters, the derision of a crow, somewhere the smack of the sea against stone. Then to Hanukkah's mild surprise a voice rose up and, with laconic precision, likened this rumored brother Alp to a secretion on the nether parts of a she-tur.

"What is your Alp to us but a galley slave?" he said.

"If he was half the man you are, boy, he would have harangued and speechified those Northmen to death weeks ago," another said.

There was laughter at this, and the soldiers felt their spirits a little restored, and little by little the square of the burned city, with its roofless mosque and its clouds of flies and its smell of death, began to resound with cries of "Filaq! Filaq!" that died away only when their object, having turned a shade of red deeper than the flush of sunset over the western gate of the town, ran down the steps of the mosque and fled into a side street.

CHAPTER EIGHT

ON A NICENESS OF MORAL DISCERNMENT UNCOMMON AMONG GENTLEMEN OF THE ROAD

They rode north through cities of carrion and widows, husk-and-stump cities where the Northmen's fires still burned. Everywhere they went—at first—male survivors of the raids fell in with the Brotherhood of the Elephant, as Filaq had dubbed them, in token of his own nickname and in bitter tribute to his dead father's fallen banner and to the creatures in whose passing lay the seeds of that fall. Some men came on horseback, bearing proper weapons, but most showed up on foot, shoeless, hungry, armed with a pruning hook or a fishing spear or the time-dulled sword of a grandfather's grandfather. Within a week of setting out for Atil, their ranks were swelled—like a gangrenous leg, as Zelikman remarked—by two or three thousand beardless fools, dodderers and men crippled by anger, aimless in their aim for revenge. Creaking leather and the snorting of mules, snatches of off-key ballads, the clop of hooves and the patter of bare soles, the rattle of hayforks and lances. In the teeming camps the nailheads of the night itself were loosened, it seemed to Amram, by snoring. They ate what they found, charred wheat in the ashes of granaries, dregs and roots and small birds. Five times a day a terrible wind blew through them and bent them like grasses to the ground.

As they moved north, synagogues began to outnumber mosques, and the towns showed no sign of ill treatment by the Rus, who had stopped only long enough to sell, peaceably, the amber, furs, timber and honey they brought with them from the north. This evident discrimination against the Muslims of the southern littoral outraged the Brotherhood, for it was seen as proof of the diabolical arrangement that the usurper, Buljan, had struck with the Northmen. And indeed, Filaq, Jew though he was, found little sympathy for his cause as they drew nearer to the capital, in the heart of Jewish Khazaria, where regard was high for the conduct and merchandise if not the uncouth manners of the Rus. Though there were expressions of regret over the reports of devastation wrought by the Northmen in the south, there was no direct experience of rapine to out-weigh the testimony of rich pelts and sweet honey and the finest Baltic amber, and anyway, it was said, every-one knew that southern Khazars were inveterate mal-contents and, furthermore, addicted to exaggeration.

"In Baghdad during the Days of Awe this year, the Muhammadans burned Jewish prayer houses and put to the sword any who would not profess Islam," they were informed by the babaghuq, or mayor, of Sam-bunin, a Jewish Khazar town only four days' ride from Atil. The babaghuq had ridden out with several city dignitaries wearing fine mustaches, backed by a well-armed if small party of soldiers, to demand the imme-diate surrender of the mutineers and to offer them, in the event they were unprepared to oblige, a generous emolument of five wagonloads of gold in the hope that the clink of dirhams might encourage the Brotherhood of the Elephant to leave Sambunin unmolested. In closing, the babaghuq quoted a remark widely attrib-uted in the north to Buljan, who claimed in turn to have only been transmitting the wisdom of the kagan, Zachariah, sequestered in his forbidden palace on his sacred island:

"If the great Caliph in Baghdad sees fit to permit

his Jews to be burned, it would be improper for the kagan of the Khazars not to ensure that his Muslims receive the same treatment."

That night in their camp on a point of land north of the ransomed city, the Brotherhood of the Elephant spitted five hundred sheep and feasted on fresh apples with honey and pistachio nuts, a parting gift of the city fathers. Zelikman had eaten little and smoked long, and now he sat staring into a campfire, stealing frequent glances toward Filaq. The Frank's unshaved cheeks sported patchy new wisps, and his golden hair hung filthy and lank.

"This is madness," he said at last.

"I agree," Hanukkah said, nodding once, taking a swallow of the tart sharab the merchants of Sambunin had been kind enough to provide. He fixed his eyes gravely on Zelikman and lowered his voice and said, "What is?"

"It's no more mad than any business we've failed at in the past," Amram said. "And maybe less. Yes, our numbers are few, if you discount the civilians—"

"As you must."

"And I do. But the fighting men are of good quality."

"True," Hanukkah said. "That is true, Zelikman. He has a point."

"And they're *angry*," Amram went on, "but not so blinded by the desire for revenge that they can't see how greatly to their advantage it will be if they can go against the hated Rus with the entire Khazar army at their backs, under the authority of a new bek. Furthermore—"

"You've constructed an argument," Zelikman observed dryly.

"I was inspired to do so," Amram said, "when I observed that you were busy constructing a funk."

"Furthermore."

"Furthermore, I hope your head is not too far inside your dudeen to notice how lightly manned Buljan's left the garrison here. They're down to half their usual strength. I'm sure the man thought he was being clever, opening the south to plunder by the Rus. Pulling their attention and their long ships away from the Crimea. Suddenly all those fat Crimean cities get left open to reconquest by Khazaria. But it looks to me now as if Buljan stretched himself a little thin across the middle."

"I imagine this is supposed to reassure me," Zelikman said, "by suggesting that Atil will be only lightly defended. And yet all it does is worry me more about the deviousness of this Buljan. These men we've gathered around us are being led to the slaughter, my friend.

And I can see no reasons for it but greed, religion and other such vanities."

"And revenge," Filaq said quietly.

"The greatest vanity of all," Zelikman said without looking at the stripling. "It's *soldiering*, Amram. I want nothing to do with soldiers, armies, chains of command. All the evil in the world derives from the actions of men acting in a mass against other masses of men."

He gathered his cloak around him and stalked off to the edge of the camp, by the tall grass at some distance from the fire, with his face turned toward Francia, a hunch in his narrow shoulders. Every so often he rose and took a few steps and muttered to himself and then sat down again.

"He is given to brooding," Hanukkah said.

"He gives me a pain," Amram said.

"He misses his home," Filaq said. "Or so he told me."

"He told you that?" Amram said, surprised. Zelikman was not a man for nostalgia or confession even under the influence of his pipe, and the scant recollections of life in Regensburg that he had offered up over the years fell well short, to say the least, of longing. "What did he say?"

"It's far, the land of the Franks," Filaq declared and then nodded sagely, as if impressed by the breadth of his own learning. He held up his hands, palms facing each other and separated by a foot of firelight. "I have seen it in a book of maps, in the library of a gentleman my father used to take me to visit."

At the mention of his father or the memory of that library with its precious maps, Filaq's soft voice turned raspy with emotion. Amram wondered if a boy holding a book of maps of the world felt as if he possessed the world and if Filaq now felt, remembering, that he had lost it. Filaq watched the brooding scarecrow alone at the edges of the dark, and an unwonted softness entered his strange green eyes. He was a hard boy, orphaned and imperious, but in the days since his momentary failure of nerve Filaq had shown clear signs to Amram of incipient fitness to command. He woke on his own in the dark of morning and retired having ensured that curfew was in force and universally observed. He held himself apart from the men as he had from Zelikman and Amram, sleeping in his own tent, performing his ablutions and elimination in private, riding usually at the head of the train with none beside him and none before, but he fell in regularly among the ranks, during the course of a day, all the way back to the weakest and most useless of the stragglers, to join them for a song or find shoes for the unshod. That afternoon he had made over his entire double share of the bribe to

"A gentleman of the road."

be divided among the feeblest and most miserable of the men. He rode well and looked fine on horseback, and he saw to it that those tending the animals were competent and humane. His authority was something bestowed by him on the Brotherhood and not the other way around, and Amram realized that he must himself have fallen to some degree under the spell of the boy's gift for being served by others, because in the light of his pessimism about the expedition there was no other explanation for his presence at Filaq's right hand, unless it was that in some inexplicable but deep-rooted way this pale-skinned, redheaded, foulmouthed young man reminded him of his dark-brown, sloe-eyed daughter, Dinah.

"What is it like, in Francia?" Filaq said, without taking his eyes off Zelikman.

"Cold and gray and green and rank with fog," Amram said. He had never seen Regensburg, but one winter long ago he had traveled up the Rhine in the retinue of the ambassador of Constantinople to the emperor of the West, and at times he felt that the chill of that journey was still in his bones. "The forests are vast and haunted by wolves and bears and men who take the shapes of wolves and bears. The cities of the Christians are mean and mildewed and devoid of splendor. They do not love Jews. Zelikman's family, learned men all, suffered persecution from mobs and princes alike."

"He is a learned man himself," Filaq said, "for a common thief."

"A gentleman of the road," Hanukkah said sternly, then winked at Amram and raised a dented tin dipper of wine. "Are we anything else?"

"Indeed we are not," Amram said, raising his own battered cup.

Filaq stood and nodded to Amram. He signaled a guard and, with a tentative hand on the man's shoulder but no hesitation in his voice, gave the order that the watch should be doubled in case soldiers from the Sambunin garrison or an assassin sent by the babaghuq attempted treachery in the night. Then he walked through the twilight to his solitary tent, picking his way carefully through the horse dung, swinging his gawky camel hips as he went.

"A curious lad," Amram said.

On the way to the tent, the youth was obliged to pass Zelikman. He stopped and stood watching Zelikman watch the light die somewhere over Francia and the West, without speaking. Zelikman seemed unaware of Filaq's presence or of the presence of anyone or anything in the world but the glowing coal of his pipe. From the tall grass beyond his partner, Amram heard a dry rasp like a rough sleeve against leather, and he was already running toward Filaq when he saw an indeterminate shiver in the air, tumbling with the slowness of dice on a mat rolling toward jackpot or ruin. Zelikman sprang up and doffed his hat like a man coming in from a long day in the sun and tossed it as if aiming for a pair of antlers on a wall. Then, as the hat, which had already known such misfortune, gave its life to deflect the flight of yet another knife, Zelikman flung himself after it, onto Filaq, who had heard and seen nothing at all. The youth looked very surprised as Zelikman came down on top of him and slammed him belly first against the ground, Filaq's chin striking with a crack. Knife and hat fell to earth like a falcon tangled with the limp bundle of its prey.

"Get off me!" Filaq said. He rolled out from under Zelikman, who looked surprised as if by the turn his bhang dream had taken. Amram kept running toward the bushes, heard thumping behind him and a moment later was overtaken by Hillel, with Filaq mounted bareback and holding Lancet like a pigsticker, charging hard into the shadows on the grass. The horse broke and feinted with deft leaps to the left and right like a ratting dog, and Filaq drove the wicked sword home. There was a cry of pain, and Filaq swung down from the horse. A handful of Arsiyah had followed their Little Elephant into the meadow, on foot and horseback, and now they fanned out looking for stray assassins. Amram ran into Filaq just as he emerged from the high grass, looking shaken, leading Hillel by the halter. He walked past Amram without a look, chest rising and falling, green eyes catching the light of the fires of the Brotherhood, and strode over to Zelikman, who had dusted himself off and was busy cutting his hat to ribbons with the assassin's knife.

"I will never again view your affection for this horse as unnatural," Filaq said, passing the lead to Zelikman. "But there is nothing to be said in favor of this blade, which is not even fit for a woman."

Filaq raised Lancet and bridged the gulf between them with its slender span, a compass needle indicating the cardinal point at the center of Zelikman's chest. They stood facing each other, separated by less distance than that which had separated Francia from Khazaria on the maps in that childhood library. There was something between them, some heat of dislike or strangled affection that Amram felt but could not understand, and he wondered if this had something to do, as well, with Zelikman's growing unease. As far as Amram knew, his partner had never lain with a woman or a man, and if he had in hard times, on cold nights, shared a companionable bed with Amram, it was a mark of how much the state of their relations resembled those between his partner and Hillel. Amram had lost much and fared widely alone, but Zelikman was simply born lonely.

Filaq wiped the blade on the flap of his tunic and then handed it back, haft first. "Thank you for saving my life," he said.

"I don't save lives," Zelikman said. "I just prolong their futility."

When the troopers returned empty-handed from hunting in the grass, Filaq ordered that word be sent to Sambunin.

"Tell them their cowardly act has failed," he said, "and that if they do not supply this noble Brotherhood with five hundred armed and able-bodied men by to-morrow morning, we will seek to test on their city the techniques we have learned from the Rus."

The tale of the failed assassination attempt was taken up within moments by the Brotherhood, and by the next day embellished word of it had spread all across the marshes. By the time the Brotherhood arrived at the gates of the city of Atil, it numbered nearly ten thousand men, including the five hundred grudged by Sambunin and four more rebel detachments of Arsiyah troops, fresh from the campaign in the Crimea, where it had been reported, with helpful inaccuracy, that a miraculous infant, accompanied by a ghost and a black giant, had raised an army and set out to conquer Khazaria and the world in the name of Allah.

The ghost in question was, however, no longer among this semi-legendary crew. He had come to Amram's tent at dawn with a cold twist of a smile on his lips.

"If I don't ask you to leave with me," he said, "it's only because I fear you'll turn me down out of sheer perversity."

"Then, by that logic, you ought to tell me to stay," Amram said.

"Stay," Zelikman said. "Fight with strangers. Die on a gate, on a rampart, in a narrow, strange street."

Amram lay back on the rough ground that had kept him awake all night and looked up at the radiance that had begun to light up the stripes of his tent.

"Maybe I'm tired," he said. "Maybe I'm tired of picking up life in bits and fistfuls and little drawstring bags. When you get to be as old as I am, there's an appeal in the idea of seeing some business through from start to finish. Besides," he said, "I don't know why, but I like the kid."

Zelikman nodded, and then they embraced and spoke some plain words in five languages, all of them roughly synonyms for farewell.

CHAPTER NINE

ON ANXIETIES ARISING
FROM THE IMPERMISSIBILITY,
HOWEVER UNREASONABLE,
OF AN ELEPHANT'S ROUNDING
OUT A PRAYER QUORUM

"War," said Joseph Hirkanos to the elephant. He spat on the grass and shook his head and pulled at the braided strands of his beard. The elephant snorted as if in agreement, with her usual air of stoic disdain, and went on ripping up sheaves of chess grass with her scarified trunk and stuffing them into her mouth. Her own warlike career long past, she was a great placid dam of at least fifty who had been captured by Normans decades ago in a raid on Muslim Sicily and fetched home to Francia to be neglected by a series of improvident barons until the day, six months ago, that she was absorbed, by way of payment, into the far-flung and arbitrary inventories of the Hirkanos clan. "Bad for the Radanites."

"Not always," said his nephew, a would-be sharp operator who lacked for the satisfaction of his ambition only the quality of sharpness and who expended all of his energies, as far as Joseph could see, on preserving his opinions from contamination by experience. "War creates opportunities too."

"In the short term," Joseph said, and spat again. "Good in the short term is always bad in the long term."

They stood on a low rise to the west of Atil, above the final bend in the tortuous road that led from the sources of the Danube, across plain and mountain and swamp, by ship and wagon, to the mouth of the Volga, a journey that had required eighteen months of hard travel. Joseph Hirkanos raised to his eyes one of those rare glasses of Persian manufacture that were a special line of his family's trade and scanned the horizon of his woes. A plume of dust half a mile tall moved against the southern sky, slow and menacing, a quill scribing oaths of rebellion along the shores of the Khazar Sea. The reports he had received, discounted by half for lies and bluster and by two-thirds for wishfulness, portrayed the rebels as a tough shank of perhaps five hundred Arsiyah horsemen seething in a thin broth of Muhammadan irregulars and pimentoed with a fistful of Nestorians, pagans, worshipers of fire and Jews who wished for or foresaw the downfall of Buljan. All of them barbarians, in the view of Joseph Hirkanos, particularly the Khazar Jews. As with most of the Turkic hordes to come tumbling on horseback out of the eastern steppe, outward forms of worship were a matter of relative indifference to the Khazars, and Joseph had always suspected that their adoption of Judaism was not the result of divine calling so much as the mark of a politic reluctance to appear to side with either their country's Christian or its powerful Muslim neighbors.

"Ten years since my last visit, and the exact moment I arrive, a war breaks out," Joseph Hirkanos said bitterly. If the Khazars, that tolerant and pragmatic people, had fallen prey to doctrinal strife, what hope was there for the world? "A *religious* war."

"That is the least of our concerns," said Menashe, his brother, appearing without a stir of air or a whisper in the grass. Like his brother and any successful Radanite Jew, he was addicted to the practice of stealth, silent and modest, fitted by training and nature to pass unremarked among the hostile and warring kingdoms except when the time came to buy or to sell, at which point, like some inverse hero in a legend, he would don his cloak of visibility and bestow the shining gift of trade on nations mired in the darkness of conquest and retaliation. "The Venetian will be dead by sunset."

They had acquired the stock and services of an Italian merchant Jew in the city of Cherson, where the father of Joseph's nephew, showing typically poor judgment, had succumbed to some kind of distemper. Now there would again be nine in their party, a situation intolerable to an observant Jew, particularly with evening coming on, though Joseph would hardly miss the Venetian's caviling or tendency to whistle tuneless tunes all day and night, even in his sleep.

"That is lamentable," Joseph said, lowering the Persian glass and looking past his brother, like him hairless and fatless, with the hooded eyes and large ears of some prudent desert mammal, past his half-orphaned half-wit of a nephew, past the huddled mules and horses, past the circle of wagons with their covers of hide and shingled plank, filled with the fortune in furs, hides, lumber, iron and gemstones that he had amassed, bartered and shepherded under so much hardship all the way from Regensburg to this windswept hillock above the lightning fork of the delta, to Atil, a city whose rulers had always displayed a notable passion for the company of elephants. "But even worse, in the eyes of the Most Holy, than the impiety of nine little Jews would be the sealing of yet another trade route from West to East because of squabbling among the faiths."

"One by one they are being lost," his brother agreed, his ancestral memory of the decline of the great age of trade fleets and caravans reaching back, like that of all Radanites, to the fall of Rome and the rise of those warring stepchildren of Judaism, the followers of Islam and Christianity, who in violation of God's desire and teaching and above all his good sense would rather kill than haggle.

"That looks like a Frank," the nephew said, and though his eyes were too young to require the optical arts of Persia and he had been born and raised among Franks, the uncles were so accustomed to ignoring his unbroken string of idiocies that neither paid the slightest attention but continued to gaze down at the shining white city of the Khazars spreading on either side of the river. By the time they turned to acknowledge the straw-haired stranger, mounted on a shaggy horse with a big nose, he was nearly upon them. Joseph just had time to note the band of pallor on the Frank's brow implying the recent loss of a hat, and the giant needle in his sword belt, which perhaps betokened membership in a mendicant order of holy haberdashers or some other monastic absurdity.

"You are Radanites," the lean-shanked stranger said in Frankish, and Joseph thought he detected a note of wonder in the stranger's voice, as if the man knew them not only by their braided beards and the style of their head wraps but had in fact met them before, in

*Neither paid the slightest attention but continued to gaze
down at the shining white city of the Khazars.*

person, somewhere among all the roads and kingdoms.
"Out of what country?"

"Francia," the nephew said, before either of his uncles could lay the silencing hand of a vague reply across
his fat fool lips. "Regensburg."

"Ah," the stranger said, and nothing more, as if the
region and the name of the city meant nothing to him,
so that Joseph's suspicions were aroused. The stranger
swung down from his saddle and stretched his legs,
making three slow circuits around the elephant, rubbing at his chin with a persuasive air of expertise,
studying the channels and sierras of her hide with his
fingertips, marking the graying stubble of her pate, the
greater involution and deeper patina of her left tooth
in comparison to the right, the skeptical cast of her
eyes.

"Cunegunde?" he said finally.

"She was known by that name at one time,"
Menashe said. "A dozen years ago, when she was part of
the menagerie of the Count Palatine of Worms."

For a moment the stranger abandoned all pretense
of wariness and stood marveling at the beast as if, in
that remote place between harsh mountains and a bar-
barian sea, he had come upon the great gray basilica of
Worms itself. Something in the stranger's face, his way
of scrutinizing the elephant as if seeing through its

rough integument to its giant organs and the ducts and sluices that served them, stirred a recollection in Joseph Hirkanos, so that he seemed, for his own part, to recognize the stranger as by a family resemblance, by the anatomist's keenness of his regard.

"Since you have risked a guess about Cunegunde, I will do the same with you," he said. "Sir, you find yourself among Jews in a piteous estate. The hour of prayer is at hand and we are but ten in number, one sick and dying from some impurity of the blood. And so I dare to inquire, in the hope that the question will not be taken amiss, if perhaps the gentleman might not count himself among the sons of Abraham and Isaac, and so make our tenth?"

The stranger said nothing, gazing up at the pachyderm, who was long overdue for a wallow, her skin dusted with scurf and the residue of travel. He sighed, and the elephant sighed, too.

"Take me to the poor bastard," the stranger said, "and I will see what I can do."

They followed the nephew to the tent, striped and bulbous like a Radanite head wrap, in which the Italian lay silvered over with perspiration, eyes open and staring like a fish's. The stranger dropped his saddlebags and called for water to be heated. He knelt and removed his outer tunic and rolled the white sleeves of the inner one. He rubbed astringent oil into his hands and along his forearms to the elbow, to the amusement of the nephew, who drew a wrongheaded moral from the notion of a physician who medicated himself and not his patient. The stranger leaned in to sniff at the Italian's breath, pressed an ear against his chest and took the poor fellow's pulse. While he worked, he asked about the stages of the Italian's illness, and about the stations of the caravan's journey, and how things fared with the Jews of Regensburg, and the condition of the roads, and whether it was true that the kagan of the Khazars might by law be seen by no one but the bek, living in imperial isolation in a palace where he reigned at once absolute and powerless for a strict term until on an appointed day he was taken into a wood and strangled with a silk garrote. The Radanites replied that they had heard the same stories with regard to the kagan, but could add little more to them without falling into the sin of wicked speech.

"I know that's the unbreakable creed of the Radanites," the stranger observed. "And yet it's a strange paradox that if one lightens a Radanite's wagons while freighting a Radanite's purse, he often finds himself in receipt of the most arrant gossip imaginable."

Menashe Hirkanos invited the stranger to repeat his question at a later juncture, perhaps after having looked over some of their stock in gems or saddlery, and see if the reply he received then struck him as more informative.

At last the stranger concluded his examination and begged them all to leave him with the patient so that he could enact, in his own dry phrase, horrible and malodorous procedures. When, an hour later, with night having fallen, the stranger joined them for the evening worship, the Hirkanoses, having compared notes in the interval, greeted him with renewed interest, which by their nature they did their best to conceal. After they remembered their dead they sat down by a good fire, and the Sorb slave piled their plates with grilled lamb and rice boiled with onion and fat and filled their cups with wine. The stranger attended to his food without apparent pleasure and sipped his wine. Then he took out a small length of clay pipe or hollowed bone, filled it with a dark paste and lit it with a straw.

"Regensburg," he said. "I spent time there, as a student of physic, many years ago. In the Jewish street."

"A golden lane of piety and learning," Joseph Hirkanos suggested, "lighting the gloomy precincts of Christendom."

"There was a family with whom I lodged. The family of Meshulem ben Hayim, noted physicians all."

Joseph, Menashe, their Hirkanos cousins and the

three other Radanites in the party, members of the Sacerdoti clan based in Ragusa, maintained the agreed-upon silence, watchful and measured. The nephew snorted and then endeavored to transform the snort into a not very credible simulation of choking on his wine.

"A great family," Joseph Hirkanos said, in the same bland way. "A credit to our brothers in the West. But not one with which we are personally acquainted, alas, having never fallen ill in that city."

"I imagine their numbers have dwindled since then," the stranger said. "They were never numerous to begin with. A few old bachelors and widowers, buried in their books. Pitiably tending to the bodies of the very nobles and burghers who condone the massacre of Jews by ignorant mobs."

"I believe," Joseph Hirkanos said, "that only one of that family remains."

"Only one."

"His name—" Joseph pretended to consult his brother with a look "—I believe it may be . . ."

"Solomon?" the stranger said eagerly, and Joseph understood for the first time how young he was. But he said nothing, and the others shook their heads in solemn ignorance or amnesia.

"You have a remarkable horse," the nephew said,

after a pause. "It's a shame that your saddle and harness are of such poor quality and so hard used."

The Radanites turned to him and stared, none longer or with more astonishment than his uncle Joseph. The stranger's puzzlement vanished more quickly than that of the Radanites.

"Indeed," he said. "I owe him better. In the morning I would like to see the best of your stock."

"Your uncle is dead," Joseph Hirkanos said. "Your father has abandoned all hope of your return."

Zelikman ben Solomon smiled.

"He abandoned that years before I ever left Regensburg," he said. "How is the old buzzard's health?"

"Weak. Once we have concluded our business in Atil, we intend to return to Regensburg, taking the more direct route. With God's help you could see him again before it is too late."

"It was too late for him and me on the day that I was born," Zelikman said.

"To forgive is a great blessing," Joseph said. "But it is a greater one still to allow oneself to be forgiven."

"The Radanite stations are comfortable and well provisioned," Menashe said. "The consideration you paid in return for passage with us would hardly reflect the luxury you could expect."

"The old boy doesn't have six months in him," the nephew said.

Zelikman thought it over, slowly, seeming to visit in his pipe fancy the fog and clear sunshine, the deep fragrant forest, the cathedral bells.

"I accept your kind invitation," Zelikman said. "My services as a physician ought just to offset my fare."

The elephant gave a low moan, startling them, and a moment later they heard a faint trill, carried on the wind from off the river, and then another.

"Trumpets," the nephew said.

They walked to the edge of the upland and saw tiny fires starring the eastern dark. The Brotherhood of the Elephant had at last arrived at the walls of Atil. Zelikman watched the pinpoints flicker with an air of uneasiness as if they formed the points of a constellation by which he hoped to steer a doubtful course.

"War," Joseph Hirkanos said. "Bad for business."

Zelikman said nothing for a long while, and the old Radanite assumed that he had not heard or had nothing to add to his sage and bitter remark.

"That's not the case, alas," Zelikman said finally, "if one is a surgeon."

The next morning, the Italian sat up and asked for broth and soon afterward was heard to whistle the opening measures of his constant tuneless tune. But when they went to find Zelikman ben Solomon of Regensburg, to thank him for saving the life of their companion, of whom, despite his whistling, they were all rather fond, neither he nor his horse could be found. A subsequent inspection of the wagons revealed the absence of a good harness and an excellent Iberian saddle.

CHAPTER TEN

ON THE BELATED REPAYMENT OF THE GIFT OF A PEAR

"I can only save men one at a time," Zelikman said.

He sat cross-legged on a carpet that smelled like rutting sheep, in the cramped gloom of a circular dog tent constructed, as far as he could tell, from equal quantities of rancid felt, dung smoke and the acrid shadow cast by a naphtha lamp. He was working to get Amram to take him and his proposal seriously, a task impeded by the fact that he was still wearing the robes and head wrap with which the Radanites had generously if unwittingly supplied him, his patchy golden beard tied in trivial plaits and blackened with lamp soot.

"I am not overly encumbered by principle, as you know," Zelikman continued. "I am a gentleman of the

road, an apostate from the faith of my fathers, a rene-
gade, a brigand, a hired blade, a thief, but on this one
small principle of economy, damn you, and damn that
troublemaking little stripling, and damn every one of
those men out there, living men, in full possession, for
the most part, of all their limbs and humors, I have to
hold firm: if we can only save them one man at a time,
then by God we must only *kill* them one man at a time."

"I didn't get a word of that," Filaq said. Having declined to sit with the reunited partners, he leaned
against the roof pole nearest the low door flap, hugging
himself in the way of a youth trying to keep his temper,
glowering at Zelikman from under his ruddy eyebrows.
"But if what this barber proposes is that, having mus-
tered these men and promised them redress of their
grievance and a fine fight, we now sneak into the city
like cutpurses and strangle Buljan in his sleep with a
silk girdle . . . "

"A scarf will do as well," Zelikman said.

" . . . and send those good men home with a hand-
clasp and our thanks for their trouble, then I suggest he
wriggle on back to whatever reeking Western sump ex-
uded him and leave us to settle this matter in the
Khazar way. Openly. By fire and steel. And soon,
Amram, today, now, before the main body of the army
can return from the Crimea and surround us."

"We sent our demand for his surrender not two hours ago, boy!" Amram said. Six lancers of the 15th Arsiyah, the best-attired, finest-armored troops in the Brotherhood, had been admitted under flag of truce into the city, bearing testimonials of the humble obeisance of the Little Elephant, Filaq, eternally loyal servant of the kagan in whose name all truces were held to be sanctified, and lenient terms of surrender to Buljan, who would be permitted to keep not only his household goods, camels and tents but—over the objections of Filaq—the eyes and tongue in his head.

"And in any case, your 'good men' have no grievance with Buljan," Zelikman said, fighting the urge to make a trial of his skill at strangulation, by scarf or bare fingers, right there. "Their quarrel is with the *Rus*. And the sooner and the easier you make yourself bek, and act to revoke the safe passage that Buljan granted to the Northmen, the sooner your men will be free to seek the redress they do want, and the more of them will live to get it. You are the one who has a grievance with Buljan, you arrogant little bastard."

"Not even in power yet and already thinking like a despot," Amram observed with a rueful smile, studying his shatranj board. "Confusing your will with the will of the men you lord it over." Without looking up from the board he grabbed at the youth's left ankle and gave it a yank, sending Filaq tumbling onto the carpet. "I swear, you are starting to worry me."

"And you are starting to worry *me*," Filaq said, scrambling to his feet, his cheeks and throat radiant with blood. "You seem to have forgotten the purpose of that impressive ax you carry about so picturesquely. I thought you were a soldier. But I see that you are just a craven barber like your friend."

"I *am* a soldier," Amram said, looking up, no longer smiling.

"Are you? Then fight like one. We should have attacked as soon as we arrived."

"The men were tired. It was dark. The city is well defended and prepared."

"Is that how they do it in the armies of Byzantium? Offer excuses in advance of the defeat, to save time later?"

Zelikman was obliged to acknowledge that Filaq had a true gift for commanding soldiers, because Zelikman knew what the stripling had intuited, namely that Amram was vulnerable to a well-timed display of taunting. The African had served too long as a pit mastiff in the dogfights of empire not to respond to an artful application of the handler's goad, even when it was wielded by a beardless youth who could have no clear notion of the hard and harrowing work that soldiering entailed. Filaq stood there with his lip curled, his pretty eyes glinting with scorn, his soft, narrow fingers playing on the hilt of his untried sword, looking as certain of victory as only a green recruit would dare.

"Let your spies within the walls do their work," Amram said. "After you have news—"

On hands and knees an Arsiyah trooper crawled in through the door flap, in a clatter of armor. He pressed his forehead to the blood-blue figured carpet and waited for Filaq to give him leave to speak.

"Has he responded?" Filaq said.

"It is—we were told that Buljan would be sending out an emissary, lord, an old friend of yours. But in the end they have sent only an elephant."

"An elephant?" Filaq whispered.

"A very old one. Thin and old and slow."

Filaq stood unmoving, shaking his head.

"It has a bald patch on its forehead," he said softly.

"Yes, lord. Spotted and hairless."

Filaq crawled past the guard, shoving him aside, and poked his head out of the door flap, looking toward the great gates of Atil. Whatever he saw when he looked out made him forget himself. He leapt up and ran, laughing, snuffling, tripping over his own feet.

Amram and Zelikman went after him and arrived before the gates just in time to see Filaq encircle with his slender arms, in their baggy sleeves of borrowed quilt armor, the gnarled proboscis of a broken-down elephant. It loomed, skeletal and listing, its skin tuberous, lumpy, pocked with whitish scars and peeling away in strips of papery excelsior that snowed and blew in little drifts around its feet: a wagonload of ragged and mildew-blown blankets hastily arranged over the staved-in ruin of a barn. A steady rattle issued from the mysterious machinery of its interior like wind in the branches of a locust tree, over a deeper rumbling, an unmistakable continuo of pleasure as the stripling rubbed at the piebald patch between its phlegmatic little eyes, gummed with a milky effluence of tears.

Filaq spoke to it, calling it his beauty and his little mother and his queen. At a slight distance from the stripling and the elephant, as if granting a measure of privacy to this reunion, the lancers of the 15th Arsiyah sat their horses, with four foot soldiers behind them bearing the flag of truce and the impromptu green *bandon* of the Brotherhood of the Elephant, the soldiers' faces expressionless and shaded by the brims of their round helmets.

The elephant withdrew its burled trunk from Filaq's embrace and turned its slow head on the scraping millstones of its vertebrae, left, right, as if indicating the men around it, producing a clucking sound with its lips or throat. It made a backward lurch toward the troopers. One of the horses shied, and its rider raised his lance and drove it deep into the flank of the elephant.

Life blew in gusts from the hole in the side of the elephant with a rank smell and a comic flatulence. It sounded a few flat whuffling notes that seemed to raise a stirring echo from far away, and then it pitched forward, its massive skull dragging it down. The architecture of the head struck the ground with a formidable tolling, but the rest of it hit with the light snap of brushwood. Its fall kicked up a roil of dust and delicate falling flakes of scurf.

"Damn me," Amram said, unslinging Defiler of All Mothers from his back. The impostors threw down the streaming banners to be trampled in the mud, unfurled the candelabrum flag of Khazaria and drew their swords. Amram reared up and began to uncoil the bite of his Viking ax, but before he had the chance to swing it, one of the impostors dragged Filaq off the body of the dead beast and, reaching for the collar of the stripling's tunic, ripped the front away, revealing a white belly with a soft prominence, a curve of hip and two yards of linen swaddling cloth wrapped tightly around a slender chest. Filaq struggled, growled, cursed and finally screamed as the soldier tore off the linen drawers, revealing a gonfalon of russet hair with nothing to inspire it but the breeze. With a flourish of his dagger—one of those bold gestures so dear to emancipators—the soldier slit the swaddling cloth, and it sprang from Filaq's body, baring the startled gaze of a pair of breasts shaped by the hand of nature to fit the cup of a lover's palm.

On that plain of mud and grass and staring faces, along the battlements and bartizans of the walls of Atil barbed with pikemen and archers, from the Black Sea to the Sea of Khazar, from the Urals to the Caucasus, there was no sound but the wind in the grass, the clop of a sidestepping horse, the broken breathing of the Little Elephant, Filaq, with whom they had marched and slept and shivered, the son, the prince they had raised up on their shoulders to rule them as their bek, the revenger of the rape of their sisters and the burning of their houses and the pillage of their goods. All Zelikman's disdain, all his resentment toward the foulmouthed spoiled stripling who had plagued him since the rescue at the caravansary vanished with the double shock of the elephant's slaughter and the revelation. In their place he felt only pity for a white thing flecked with mud, a motherless girl, drooping in the grip of the soldier like a captured flag.

Before Amram could recover, the mounted impostors had him at the point of their lances. He studied the angles and distances, the lean faces under the helmets, the wonder of the girl, the glinting steel tips of the lances. He threw down his ax. They bound his arms behind him, and with the girl they drove him toward the gates of the city. Zelikman reached for Lancet, but as if he had heard the snick of the blade Amram whipped his head around, seeking among the baffled faces of the Brotherhood for his old friend's, and in his own impassive mien there was neither a warning against hasty action nor the fatalism of defeat but a hint of amusement more useful and wise: *Can you top this?* And Zelikman recollected his own intelligence, forgot his outrage, resisted the urge to act in panic and left his blade where, for now, it belonged.

Like apes on a rock at sunset, like crows in the trees, like the bells in the watchtowers of a city under attack, the men of the Brotherhood fell to talking all at once, as those nearest the gates and those at the extremes of the encampment sought to reconcile the stark prodigies of observation with the grandiose inventions of rumor.

"Master?" Hanukkah said, approaching Zelikman warily, one hand extended like a man searching out a stairhead in the dark. He wore a mail shirt and one boot and no pants, with his arm in a sling and a bruise on his cheek, a hangover folded about him like a cloak, tottering, squinting, a loop of his woolen bedroll caught in a link of his mail so that the blanket dragged along behind him in the mud. "Is that you?"

And he reached out, his pudgy cheeks slack, his bright little eyes drained by surprise of any visible emotion, to tug at one of the braids of Zelikman's beard. But the day was not yet replete with wonders, because before Zelikman could reply there were shouts from the rear and then the blatting tantara of an inhuman horn. A fissure opened in the mass of soldiers, and like a dike giving way before the ransacking arm of a flood they fell back or ran to get out of the path of Cunegunde, the elephant, who came shambling toward the gates of Atil, her hide scrubbed, oiled and glistening in the sun, caparisoned in purple silk and cloth of gold, the tips of her tusks capped with gilded leather sheaths. On her back in a large rush basket jostled the nephew of Joseph Hirkanos with three or four of his uncles, clutching the sides of the basket. The effect of the fine silk robes they wore, like that of the bright ribbon braiding their beards and moustaches, was spoiled to a degree by the expressions of terror on their faces as she ran wild.

Cunegunde stopped beside the body of the dead elephant, and stared at it with an unreadable expres-

A fissure opened in the mass of soldiers.

sion. She snuffled, and rumbled, and investigated its sounds and the pocks and scars of its hide. She redistributed her weight impatiently among the pillars of her frame, and some fundamental injustice or harsh fact about the world seemed to confront her afresh, with no gain in meaning or message. The dead animal was a distant cousin to her at best, Zelikman supposed, no nearer kin than Amram was to him.

Zelikman clapped Hanukkah on the shoulder and then ran toward the elephant. The Radanites riding in the howdah, not yet fully recovered from their jaunt, appeared taken aback by the sudden appearance, amid the legs of their merchandise, of one of their own guild. Even Joseph cried out in alarm as Zelikman grabbed hold of one of the gilt-embroidered purple strips that fluttered from the withers of the elephant and used it as a rope to pull himself up to the shoulders of the beast, whom his disguise neither alarmed nor, apparently, deceived. Twenty years earlier, at the St. John's Fair at Mainz, a Jewish boy sneaked into the stall where the elephant was kept for the night and fed her a ripe pear, and patted her flank, and spoke a kind word in the holy tongue, which he believed at the time to have been the original language of elephants and men, and now, when that boy, grown to a man, lost his footing on the elephant's flank and began to slide down the silken panel to the ground, Cunegunde reached back and, with the tip of her trunk against the seat of his breeches, held him steady until he could regain his purchase.

"The offer to join us was a simple one, really," Joseph Hirkanos said when Zelikman tumbled into the basket, looking him up and down from the tips of his curled slippers to his blackened hedgehog of a plaited beard to the clumsy windings of his head wrap. "But I divine that you find a way to complicate everything."

CHAPTER ELEVEN

ON THE UNFORESEEN AND ANNOYING RESEMBLANCE OF A BEK'S LIFE TO AN ILL-PLAYED GAME OF SHATRANJ

At the Feast of Booths it was the custom of the beks of Khazaria to pitch their leaf tents in the yard of the prison fortress called Qomr, a mound of yellowish brick rising up from the left bank of the turbid river, in whose donjon by long tradition the warlord was obliged to lay his head. But on his return to Atil from the summer hordes, the usurper Buljan ordered that his sukkah be erected on the donjon's roof, with its strategic views of the kagan's palace, the seafront, the Muslim quarter and the steppe, and above all with its relative nearness to the stars, among which his sky-worshiping and uncircumcised ancestors still hunted with infallible gyrfalcons for celestial game.

When Sukkot ended, he declined to dismantle the

booth and, after a one-sided consultation with the grand rabbi, took his wife and three daughters to dwell there with him. Whispers began that a guilty conscience was preventing the new bek from taking up residence in the royal apartments, and even that the ghost of his murdered predecessor in phantom rags had been seen in the donjon's upper windows. But the truth was that Buljan found comfort in the sukkah, in this open-air proof of the affinity between his own fathers and those of the people (by the account of their own book once a wandering horde of tent dwellers and cattle raiders) whose faith they had adopted. The new bek's great-grandfather had passed every night of his life under the sky, on the back of a pony or in the felt walls of a ger, and Buljan retained the ancestral contempt for cities and city dwellers. He could not contemplate the move indoors without experiencing a panic in his skin.

"The fate of the Khazars appears to have become curiously knit up with the fate of its elephants," he said to the strange Radanite agent, who sat on the carpet, crosslegged, under the interlaced rushes of the roof. Buljan himself perched on the tripod of his office, formed from gilded elks' antlers, with his bekun beside him nursing his infant and his twins playing in the corner with colored beads and some squirrels' tails. The girls, not yet fluent in the holy tongue, looked up at the word *elephants*. "We must therefore be grateful to you for having helped us begin to restore our herd. I am personally very pleased."

"Then we have fulfilled our sole ambition," the Radanite replied, having apologized for the insufficiency of his Khazari. "An animal, by the way, of excellent character."

Buljan reached toward the shatranj board at his right hand, picked up one of the alfils of dark green stone, then set the jade elephant down again. He expected at any moment to receive, via armed guard, the response of the prisoner in the south bastion to his most recent move. The bek's position looked strong, but in his belly he felt the clutch of a fist and knew that he was in trouble from some quarter of the board. He had the kind of bravery—the most effective kind—that derives from playing only when one is assured of victory. He anticipated arrival of the armed guard with unwonted dread.

"Character?" he said, signaling to the Sorb slave who waited, shivering, outside the booth. The day was bright and the sky as blue as the beard of his great-grandfather's God, but the wind was cold and had a smell of rusty iron. "In this town that will be an anomaly."

Head bowed, silenced forever at the root of the

tongue by the bek's own dagger, the Sorb entered the booth bearing a steaming copper pot and poured into the bek's cup more of the infusion of dried camellia leaves, imported from Khitai at great expense, on which Buljan depended to keep up his spirits in the city. "Find me one more honest creature living in Atil and I will have myself a pair."

The agent only nodded his head and smiled a Radanite smile, which was not a smile at all but rather a promissory note to deliver one at some unspecified future date. He was a bony-faced fellow with light eyes, younger than the usual old rug dealer, the jet of his mustache and skimpy beard plaits contrasting starkly with his fair skin.

"People saw the deaths of the previous elephants as an ill omen for their custodian," Buljan continued, lowering the brim of his hat over his eyes. The hat was a fine piece of workmanship, also from Khitai, yak felt covered in panels of ultramarine silk embroidered in black and silver, but, crippled by headaches that made him sensitive to light, Buljan prized it chiefly for its wide brim. "One that proved accurate, which in my experience does not often happen with omens."

The Radanite was peering at the board, and though he quickly returned his gaze to Buljan, the latter did not fail to remark the scintilla of understanding in the merchant's eyes. Whatever fate awaited Buljan on the shatranj board, this Radanite saw it.

"We of course had heard nothing about the recent changes in your government," he said. "When we arrived and learned of the precarious situation, particularly here in the Qomr, our anxiety on your behalf was considerable."

"I should imagine so," Buljan said, taking the infant from the bekun so that she might cover her breast. "And I look forward to perusing your stock."

As if this were a signal, the Radanite started to rise, more willing than most of his kind to show that he was eager to conclude business. Buljan glanced at his wife, who raised an eyebrow at this atypical display of haste.

"I can spare you very little time," Buljan said, rocking the baby with an audible slosh of the milk in its belly, resisting an urge to question the Radanite about his predicament on the shatranj board. Since wresting control of the bek's tripod, a measure he took only after concluding that a coup was not just necessary and advantageous to himself and his clan but also likely to succeed, he had experienced only doubt, rumor and rebellion. His solace, apart from sleeping in the tent of leaves, had been a strict policy of playing shatranj with opponents he knew he could defeat. "But surely not so little as that."

"Please," the bekun said, holding out a silver plate on whose border running horses were chased in gold. She was a Rus, with copper hair and golden eyelashes. "Another sweet?"

The Radanite lowered himself back to the carpet and took another little pellet of the paste of honey, roses and almond oil.

"The premises are rather full, I imagine," the Radanite said, glancing back at the inlaid board.

"To the rafters," the bek said. "Thanks to the recent foolishness."

"No doubt it was foolish, even demented, to unite behind the banner of an untried female, my lord. But one can hardly have expected the Muhammadans to enjoy the treatment they received at the hands of the Rus."

"Nor did I so intend," Buljan said. "This empire is only as strong as its neighbors are weak. My predecessor coddled our Muhammadans, granting them so many privileges that they grew too strong, encouraging the caliph's northern hopes. And he all but ceded the Crimea to the Rus. He was mistaken in nearly all his policies, while the only mistake I made was failing to clean house properly. That has now been remedied. The common rebels I will permit to return to their homes and vineyards—or what remains of them. The mutinous Arsiyah will be dealt with appropriately."

"How sad," the Radanite said. "That really is, if I may say, my lord, a remarkable hat."

Buljan stared at the Radanite, wondering what it was, aside from the madness of power, that had persuaded him that his destiny lay not on the open steppe but amid the meshes of the shatranj board that was city life.

"It pains my uncle greatly that he is unable to treat with you in person, my lord," the Radanite said. "But it was felt that I should come in his stead as soon as possible." He glanced at the board again, and hesitated. "One hears rumors of a giant African."

"An enormous fellow," Buljan said, understanding now. "A prodigy. Powerful. Well favored. Intelligent too." He felt relief as the nature and mission of his interlocutor became clear to him. "It is a long time since we have had any slave-dealing Radanites in Atil. We heard your people had forsworn the trade in men."

"News can be slow to diffuse among my people," the Radanite said apologetically, crinkling the corners of his eyes in a show of slyness.

"How fortunate for you."

"May I—would it be possible, I wonder, to see this prodigy for oneself?"

Before Buljan could reply, a guard entered and bowed, his face expressionless, having no understanding of, or interest in, the words he was about to pronounce.

"The prisoner moves his vizier to the seventeenth square, my lord, and respectfully offers you the opportunity to concede the game."

With a distinct thud, Buljan, blind, dissolved in an impenetrable night of rage, dropped the baby onto the rug. The little girl screamed, and the mother screamed, and the twins gazed at their father as if he had just burst into flame.

"His life is not for sale," Buljan said. He picked up the baby and handed it to his wife without a glance. "But it will cost you nothing to see it spilled into the dust."

Under the windows of the donjon, to the very spot in the courtyard on which previous beks had put up their harvest booths, a detachment of six well-armed guards escorted the African. He was stripped to the waist, with his hands lashed behind his striped and bleeding back, his eyes fixed steadily before him.

A dozen carpenters carried in sawed planks and stout posts, and with hammers, pegs and thongs quickly assembled a wide table onto whose top two large blocks of wood were fixed on either side of center. Four grooms led in the horses, harnessed as for plowing, and then the African was asked, with fitting tenderness, to lie on his back between the blocks, which were intended to hold his torso in place as the horses disjointed him and carried his limbs to the corners of the yard, but the blocks proved to have been set too close to admit the span of his great back.

"What an appallingly inefficient way to kill a man," the Radanite said, standing beside Buljan on a terrace overlooking the yard.

"What's that?" Buljan said.

"His offense was great, I will allow," the Radanite said. "But surely not so great as the bek would show himself to be in having the mercy to permit me, with every assurance that the African will be sold to an exacting and implacable master, to purchase him."

One of the carpenters had fetched a crowbar and set about prying loose the blocks.

"And what do you imagine, Radanite, his offense to have been?"

"Rebellion. Insurrection."

"But he is not a Khazar subject." And Buljan smiled, knowing it was foolish but enjoying nonetheless the sensation of puzzling one of that enigmatic tribe. "How could he then rebel? No, those are not the grounds of his punishment."

The Radanite watched as the African was introduced successfully between the blocks, on either side of his rib cage, and as a horse was tightly cinched, by the reins of its harness, to each of his ankles and wrists. The African's face remained impassive; he seemed already to have crossed into the world of his ancestors. But something about the procedure appeared to trouble the Radanite, and his attention seemed to be focused on a particular horse, a bandy-legged, shaggy freak of a tarpan with a prominent nose.

"He beat you at shatranj," the Radanite said with gratifying wonder in his voice.

"Nonsense," the bek said. "I never lose at shatranj."

He turned to one of his guards and extended a gloved hand. The guard brought forward the African's ax, and the bek hefted it.

"What would you give me for this?" he said. "I am sure it would fetch a good price for you farther down the road. After I have used it to disembowel its former owner, I will make a present of it." He turned it over and ran his fingers along the runes. "I wonder what they say."

"I can tell you that," the Radanite said, and translating freely into surprisingly good Khazari he shoved

He turned it over and ran his fingers along the runes.
"I wonder what they say."

Buljan with his shoulder and snatched the ax. He leapt onto the balustrade of the terrace and as Buljan regained his feet cried out a word that sounded like a name, cried out from the depths of his soul: "Hillel!"

The shaggy horse reared and beat a tattoo on the skull of the carpenter who was tying him to the African's right leg, tore loose and charged across the yard. Just before the Radanite leapt he turned to Buljan and frowned as if trying to make up his mind. A moment earlier it would have been hard for Buljan to conceive of an astonishment greater than that which he already felt, but it was nothing compared with his surprise when the Radanite grabbed his embroidered silk hat. Then he leapt into space.

He landed with a grunt of pain athwart the horse's back and drove toward the giant, who was already employing his freed leg to kick at the line that bound his right one. The Radanite described a wild circuit around the table, slashing the cords with the ax blade, knocking aside the carpenters with the butt of the handle. By the time Buljan had recovered wit enough to give the order to stop them, the African was mounted bareback on one of the other horses, reunited with his ax, and the Radanite, clutching the silken headache hat, had gotten hold of a pike. The riders circled each other for a moment and then turned their mounts and rode for the gate of the yard.

Buljan leapt over the side of the terrace now, pushed one of his guards from a horse and took off across the yard, calling in his confusion for a volley from the archers on the roof. The troops who followed him shied and reined their horses in, and one of the black-fletched arrows lodged with a humming snap in Buljan's shoulder as he followed the African and the Radanite through the gate, along the ringing cobbles into the porter's hall, cool, dank, with sparks from the hooves of the African's mount lighting up the dimness.

When Buljan emerged into Fortress Street and the migraine blaze of day, just before he tumbled in a swoon from his horse, he remarked the fat little deserter he hired to hunt down the daughter of his predecessor, hopping alongside a mule with one foot caught in the stirrup. Buljan rose from the ground, reached over the top of his back and yanked out the arrow with a nauseous wet pop that sent him again to his knees.

After being dragged along Fortress Street, the fat little deserter managed to mount his mule and went after his confederates, whooping like an idiot, the false Radanite trailing the unraveling banner of his head wrap and waving the purloined hat in the air, the

African slinging his ax across his back, alive, bound for the open steppe and the infinite endless tracks that crosshatched it.

"Wait," said the bek of Khazaria, with a plaintiveness that surprised him. "Wait, you bastards."

CHAPTER TWELVE

ON A CONSIGNMENT
OF FLESH

"He is in love with a hat," said Flower of Life, frowning at Zelikman through the crook of Amram's arm.

Amram sat propped on an elbow, on a cloak spread across the timbered floor of her cubicle, admiring her. Her skin was of a smokier hue but as dark as his, and if she was younger than Amram she was not quite young, and at any rate the world and all its sorrows were younger than Amram, or so it felt to him, and when he studied the lines at the corners of her eyes and mouth he said to himself that his wife, had she lived, might have come to bear such a face.

"If so," Amram said, somewhat weary of the matter of Zelikman and hats, "it would not be the first time."

It was the profoundest hour of the night, their third as inmates of Princess Celestial Hind's dosshouse, a converted wool factory fronting on an alley off Sturgeon Street, not far from the Caspian wharfs. Stars at the narrow window, cicadas in the boxwood of the garden, from some other part of the house the sobbing of a bowed rebab, at the far end of the garden a brokenhearted wife or mother wailing for a dead man in the street. The wind from the steppe took up and carried off like booty the stench of the burned city, burned horsehair and plaster, burned carpets, the burned timbers of the bridge that joined the Khazar town on the left bank to the town of Muslims and foreigners on the right.

For two days and nights, since rumors first stole across the bridge with whispers of five hundred rebel Arsiyah put to death in the yard of the Qomr, the fugitive partners had been trapped by riot and counterriot with fifteen whores, male and female, among them Hanukkah's beloved Sarah; the procuress Celestial Hind, supposedly a bastard half-sister of the kagan; a cat; a weasel; and an ill-tempered macaque called Fortunatus, a name that delighted Amram, being "Zelikman" put into Latin.

"He won't drink," Flower of Life observed.

She was a slave who claimed to originate among a wandering eastern people skilled at chiromancy called the Atsingani, a claim that Amram rather doubted since he had never heard of the Atsingani and he could not believe that any race that produced such fine-looking women could long escape the notice of the world.

"He prefers his pipe."

"He will not sport with the girls."

"Never."

"Nor with the boys."

"No. Just count yourself fortunate," Amram said, "that he has yet to regale you with accounts of the horrors he has seen wrought by pox on the organs of love."

"Then tell me," she said, sitting up now to get a better look at Zelikman where he sat curled into himself on the window ledge, turning the hat over and over in his hands, studying the legend of embroidered vines as if it contained the answer to a riddle. "What is the matter with the man?"

"He feels remorse. He is sad."

She thought it over and rejected it with a shake of her long head.

"I still say he is in love, and maybe not with a hat."

"Highly doubtful."

"Are you sad? Filled with remorse?"

"I've lost the knack," Amram said. This was far from the truth and yet not entirely a lie. In the back

GENTLEMEN OF THE ROAD

garden, amid the boxwood and blackberry and half-wild grape vines, the splintered, staved-in remains of a teamster's cart, left over from the days when this had been the residence of Georgian wool factors, bore witness to the fury with which Amram and Mother-Defiler had greeted the news of the massacred men in the Qomr. But that was two days ago. He didn't want to think about the murdered troops anymore, or the big-mouthed stripling of a girl who had been their general. So he had failed to protect Filaq, and to keep his word to the poor dead mahout with his one eye and his ancient sword and his ever-suitable sneer. Amram had been living with the knowledge of failure all his adult life, since the day his daughter went down to the reeds of the river Birbir with a basket of laundry and never returned. That was Dinah's fortune. And what befell Filaq was Filaq's fortune, as failure was his; failure, and a hard-won knowledge of the immutability of Fortune itself. The hell with it. He drew back Flower of Life's hair from her cheek. "But I might be sad when I have to leave your arms."

"Oh, ho. Very fine. But you can't leave."

"Not with a company at every city gate."

"Where would you go if you could leave?"

Amram thought it over and felt a seam open onto a void whose terrible content was the possibility that there was nowhere new for him to wander, no corner where he had not sought the shadow of his home and family.

"It doesn't matter where you go, does it, not when you have a hat like that," Amram said, wincing at the clank of false cheer in his tone. "Isn't that right, Zelikman?" In fact even if he were not a fugitive from the bek, and the streets not plied by creaking wagons bearing away the bodies of rioters and civil guards, Amram might have been content to remain as he was for a week or a month, in the company of Flower of Life, who had treated his wounds and relieved his sundry appetites, and sung him violent ballads in strange keys, all for a reasonable fee. "Give that boy a handsome bonnet and a good horse and he will make his bed on a grill over the Adversary's own cook-fire, won't you, friend?"

Zelikman said nothing for a long time, long enough that Amram lay back on the figured carpet, stretched out with his head in the lap of Flower of Life and closed his eyes, and nearly forgot that he had even asked a question.

Zelikman tossed the hat to the floor as if it, too, had been holed through the crown by a thrown dagger.

"It's only a hat," he said at last, his voice lost in a gloom as dense and chill as those that afflicted his homeland.

Amram sat up, alarmed, resigned and irritated all at once, knowing that there was a correct thing to be done and that they must now do it, if only to put Zelikman out of his misery once and for all.

"All right," he said, "all right, damn you to hell, Zelikman, we'll go after her."

At this moment there was a pounding on the heavy oak door downstairs, and a commotion among the girls and boys on the second floor where trade was conducted, and then they heard the querulous voice of the procuress. Amram reached for his sword. His partner slid from the window ledge and grabbed the old curved shank with which Hanukkah had armed him, Zelikman having left Lancet in the care of the Radanites at the hostel when he set off four days ago to try to purchase Amram's freedom. Amram considered a leap through the window, into the garden, but in the end his curiosity won and he crept down the stairs to the lower landing.

Two soldiers in armor stood in the hall, settling with the procuress the fate of a slim, pale girl in a thin wrapper of muslin, all elbows and knees, her close-cropped hair the red of a sorrel horse. Her head hung down and her shoulders were hunched, her arms bound at the wrists with a length of silk cord. She stared at the floor while terms were contracted for her indenture to

Two soldiers in armor stood in the hall.

the House of Princess Celestial Hind on Sturgeon Street, with a percentage to be paid every month in gold dirhams to a certain gentleman whose name need not be mentioned and who, let it be known, had recovered swiftly from his injury, the severity of which rumor had greatly exaggerated.

As soon as the door was bolted behind the soldiers, whom the procuress had encouraged to depart with the offer of a gratis hour when they came off duty in the company of the best fare her poor house could offer, Zelikman pressed past Amram and hurried to the girl. He stood hesitating for an instant, looking her up and down, taking in her dull gaze and broken stance, and though the hesitation was not unexpected it so lacked his partner's usual bright detachment, it brimmed so with pity and regret, that Amram had to look away. Then Zelikman used the knife to cut the silk cord, put his arm around her shoulders, ignoring the flinch from the girl's arms, and asked if she thought she could walk up two flights of stairs to a room that was quiet and where, after he had cared for her, she could be alone, or in company, whichever she preferred.

She did not reply at first and seemed not to have heard or understood, and for a moment Amram feared that her soul had been damaged in some irreparable way. But then she raised her head, cheeks bearing the

swollen imprint of the hand of a man, and saw Zelikman and Amram and the monkey and the whores all
staring at her like a prodigy fallen from a cloud and
open to a number of dire interpretations. She grabbed
at Zelikman's sheltering arm as if to push it away, then
changed her mind and took hold of his hand, and nodded.

"I need you to put me back together," she said. "I
have a man to kill."

He led her up the stairs by the hand and Amram
followed, with Flower of Life carrying a basin of hot
water and some slashed bedsheets on a battered tin
tray. Amram spread the billowing cloak over the
whore's pallet and they laid the girl down. Zelikman
suggested that her treatment might require removing
her shift and the girl Filaq said in a burst of harsh
Khazar that he should damn well do what he needed
to do.

Her flesh was grilled with scratches and bright lac-
erations, bruised and striped. On her pale thighs caked
streaks of brown blood drew a soft moo of pity from
Flower of Life. Zelikman wrung a rag over the basin
and cleaned her insofar as such a thing was possible of
the stain of her deflowering and of the grime and filth
of the Qomr. He bathed her feet, her knees, her neck,
working quickly and silently and with no more tender-

ness than he would have shown to a stranger or a horse, which was not to say none at all, indeed far from it; but his characteristic coolness of manner as a physician seemed to return to him with the revelation of the slight frame and the injuries of the girl.

"This will sting," he told her, fingers greased with a paste he had concocted from fat and honey and the scanty store of herbs and perfumes the whorehouse kept on hand.

"Good," she said.

When he was through he wrapped her in a blanket and fed her from a chipped clay bowl, and she was asleep, sitting up, before half the thin soup of peas and mutton was gone. The next morning she woke and ate steadily and wordlessly for half an hour, and when she had wiped her mouth she asked for a pair of breeches and a tunic, and pronounced herself healed and only in want of a sword.

"We're glad to hear it," Amram said, "but Zelikman and I have talked it over and come to the conclusion that you can't possibly kill Buljan in his present estate. He is too powerful, too strong, too well protected and too well armed. I understand that you want revenge, Filaq. It is an impulse I know and respect. But it must not be heeded. It must be deferred. Now I can see that you're about to open that big mouth of yours and pro-

MICHAEL CHABON

nounce the word 'coward,' and so I have to warn you
that if you offer such a mistaken analysis of my character and that of my friend, who though admittedly
prone to brooding and self-doubt is braver than any
man I have ever known, excepting myself, I will be
under an immediate obligation to kick your narrow
pink ass."

She hugged herself and went to the narrow window, the legs of the leather breeches whispering as she
crossed the room. She looked out at the overgrown garden, the rusty red leaves of the grapevines, the steely
sky, the smoke of the fires that would not go out. Then
she turned back to the partners.

"So we must first find a way to change Buljan's estate," she said.

"That was our thought," said Amram.

"We don't claim to understand this doubled king-
ship that you live under," Zelikman said. "It strikes us as
overelaborate."

"It strikes me as stupid," Amram said. "Correct me
if I have it wrong. As far as I can tell, the bek runs the
country, and the army, and the treasury; but the kagan
runs the bek."

"The kagan rarely speaks," the girl said. "But when
he does his word is sacred. Inarguable. Absolute."

"That's the man we want to see," Amram said.

CHAPTER THIRTEEN

ON SWIMMING TO
THE LIBRARY AT THE HEART
OF THE WORLD

A cross a river frozen to the depth of a planted spear, along an avenue of blazing torches, drawn by reindeer in a royal sledge with fittings of mica and electrum, accompanied by ram's-horn blasts and harness bells and the scrape of iron runners against the ice; tender contraband, hidden at her father's side in the grandiose reek of a bearskin, with the heat and the weight of him against her and the full moon hanging minted against the sky like a bright dirham: that was the way she had last crossed over to the island of the kagan and the palace where he dwelt in friendless splendor. Now she crossed in utter dark, swimming the river at the last hour of night, naked and freezing, preserved from drowning only by the saving company of gentlemen of the road fated someday to be hanged. Greased with tallow, sidearms strapped to their backs, their clothes tied around their necks in bituminized bladders, huffing, gasping. The river in autumn still flowing swift and in its motion burning colder than ice. When she first slipped into the water on the Khazaran side she felt panic, iron bands and deadweights on her chest and ankles, and then numbness like a toxin in her muscles, a fatal resignation. And then Zelikman's hand reaching for her, dragging at her wrist, shoulder, hair, his voice at once harsh and tender hissing, *Swim you lazy bitch.*

At the southern tip of the island that was shaped like a letter *qof* they splashed up a stone embankment and clambered stiff and stumbling like unarticulated iron beings. Unslinging their sacks, they rolled in the grass and shadows of a laurel grove in which, so her father had told her, a kagan new-crowned was forced to his knees and informed, with his neck in the loop of a silken garrote, of the precise day and hour on which he would be returned to the spot and dispatched, by a slip-knot, to the afterlife of kings.

Cold humming in her, she dressed hurriedly and led Amram and Zelikman up out of the grove and along the scarp toward the southern or Bee Gate. A peacock screamed. The river rang and chuckled. On the right bank they could see the infernal orange of burning houses, and outlined against the glow the sleeping black cat of a mosque. Beyond the scarp rose a flight of broad stone stairs called the Bee Steps, and then they struck the south gate, stout timbers set into an arch in the circular wall, a massive thing of Byzantine plan promising impregnability but untested by war or engine in all the long years of peace.

Into the massive oak portal a man-size door was cut, and it was through this that the guardsmen charged with defending the gate passed to stand their watches. They were six stout Colchian Guards, black-armored, spread out around the door in the gate. Stamping their feet, asleep with their eyes open, dour mountaineers married to silence and solitude. In her mind she sketched the path that she would cut, if she had to, if she could, if only they would let her, she and her borrowed inferior sword, swinging the blade, whirling, lunging, a zigzag path like the lacing of a buskin. But her life and her actions were never her own and never had been from the first hour of her consciousness and so she left the sword in its scabbard and watched, scowling, as Zelikman, wrapped in black from head to toe, crept up behind the Colchians one by one and fed them through the nostrils one of his magical drafts. They sank to their knees with audible sighs like cursed men released from a spell. She followed Amram out of the shadows and watched impatiently as he used the edge of Mother-Defiler to prize open the door in the gate.

She had always found a paradox in the crime of blasphemy, for it seemed to her that any God who could be discountenanced by the words of human beings was by definition not worthy of reverence, but even to pass through the Bee Gate into the Alley of Bees was a terrific profanation and perhaps it was the lingering chill of the river in her bones but she thrilled with her first few steps.

They were surprised at the next gate by a huge Turkoman who came out of nowhere, the skin of a tiger knotted by its paws around his shoulders, and lunged at Amram with a steel lance. It passed through the quilting of Amram's bambakion and struck the mail he wore underneath with a muffled spark like a lamp flickering behind a curtain. She flung herself onto the Turkoman's back and with the rank bacon smell of his oiled hair in her nostrils bit off his ear, a salt apricot between her teeth. She had her thumbs in the Turkoman's eyesockets but before they could know that burst of hot immersion Zelikman was there with his reeking rag and the man drained to the ground like sand running out of an hourglass.

Zelikman shook his head, wearing a look of re-
proach, and in answer she spat the hunk of ear at his
feet and kept on walking, aware as she moved forward
of a rushing in her head like a swell of fervent chanting,
a wobble in her ankles. She could feel the green tendrils
of the sleeping draft twining up the doorposts of her
mind. She listed to the side and slammed her shoulder
against a stone pillar. Amram caught her and set her on
her feet, and Zelikman laid his cold fingers along her
temples, and she came to herself. But the remainder of
the journey to the apartments of the kagan partook of
the labyrinthine tedium of a dream, and she was never
afterward able to recall it, or to say how, in the darkness, with her last visit to the palace having occurred in
her girlhood, with her mind disordered by the draft
and the iron flavor of blood in her mouth, she managed
to conduct the thieves, with accuracy and haste, to the
heart of the heart of her world.

It was just as she remembered it, as in her dream, as
in any dream: a circular brick tower on a miniature islet
of brick, in a glossy black moat, within a ring of laurels,
at the center of a vast courtyard of cyclopean flagstones, at the very midpoint of the city of Atil and the
Palace of the kagan. Imposing and forlorn, a grave
marker, a dolmen, the eyrie of some august raptor. At
the top four timbered loggias each carved with the

totem animal of the direction it faced (raven, dove, bee, heron); at the base a narrow doorway. Here four more Colchians stood guard and here Zelikman found that he had run out of narcotic elixir, so that to gain entrance the partners, showing the same maddening restraint they seemed to feel was incumbent upon them as her "guardians" now that she had been exposed as a female, albeit one who would in a transport of impatience chew off a man's ear, were obliged to employ the haft of the ax, the flat of a sword and an admittedly impressive display of simple pounding with fists and boot heels.

A commotion was therefore unavoidable, and by the time they had wound, like the ant of Daedalus threading the conch, up the involute stairway to the highest chamber in the city of Atil, the kagan was on his feet and waiting for them, wearing a hard little smile, as if the whole adventure from the meeting with the partners at the caravanserai until now, as if all that slaughter and struggle had been arranged beforehand or at least foreseen by this tall, fat man with the cropped hair and the beard close-trimmed over pitted jowls and the eyes so mournful, tender, pitiable and pitying that she could not meet them.

"The little mouse," he said.

Grief swelled her chest and throat as if the iron

A commotion was therefore unavoidable.

bands of the river had finally snapped. The kagan opened his hands and turned them palm upward as though testing for rain. Waiting for her. And though no one had touched him or even looked him in the eye in thirty years she went to him, and after a moment of uncertainty he transgressed all laws and took her stiffly in his arms, and in a whisper he called her by the name that apart from her brother he alone now knew out of all the men and women on the face of the earth.

It was a while, a longer time than they could afford, before she could arrest the sobs that shook her, draw her sword and lay the point of it against one of the luxuriant folds of his throat.

"Buljan dies or you do," she informed him.

"Show some ambition, little mouse," the kagan said, looking not at the blade but into her eyes. "Why settle for one or the other?"

"Girl," Amram said. "Lower your sword."

She dipped the tip of the blade to the kagan's belly and then returned it to the scabbard slung across her shoulders. Zelikman had his back to all of them, stalking a long shelf of folios and scrolls with his fingers flickering at his sides as if he longed to touch them. Apparently he had no particular interest in meeting or even noticing one of the three princes acknowledged as a peer by the Emperor of Byzantium, along with the Emperor of the Franks and the Caliph of Baghdad.

"We're marked," she said. "Hunted."

"I know," the kagan said.

"I've lost everything."

"I know it, little mouse."

He pointed to the only seat in the room, a low couch covered in dappled ponyskin. She shook her head.

"These two . . ."

"Have nothing to lose?" He spoke in the holy tongue. "Amram, isn't it? An Abyssinian. I am pleased. I have never seen an African in the flesh before." Amram touched his forehead. "I perceive that you served in the army of my brother emperor. I have heard a good deal about that ax you carry. Tell me, have you ever used it to shave the throat of one of the princes of the earth?"

Amram shook his gray head. "Only a petty one," he said. "A minor khan or two."

The kagan looked delighted by this information. He turned to Zelikman and spoke a careful sentence in an outlandish tongue. Zelikman replied in the same language, lightly, then spun around, the yellow curtain of his hair flying. He stood for a moment blinking at the kagan. Then he swept the pretty embroidered hat from his head and bowed low.

The kagan conversed with him a little in the language of Zelikman's unimaginable homeland, a dense jargon that seemed to her to be pronounced with the front and the back of the tongue at the same time, and with the lips simultaneously pursed and opened wide. Then he went to the shelf and took down a large vellum book and handed it to Zelikman.

"The *De Urines* of Alexander Trallianus!" Zelikman said. "But it was lost."

"Imperfectly."

Zelikman took the book with reverence and set it on a lectern and started to turn its pages, and she supposed that they had lost him now for a long time.

"So you know a lot," Amram said. "Do you know what this girl wants, and how she can get it?"

"That depends. Do you want to be the bek, little mouse?"

She shook her head. "I knew it would not work," she said. "So in my heart I never desired it. Not for myself. For my brother, yes. For Alp. And I still want to drive Buljan from the tripod, and hold it for Alp until he can be ransomed or liberated. And then we will see to the Rus. And if a woman may not be bek there is no law, so far as I know, to prevent her from becoming a tarkhan. I have already proved that I can lead soldiers into a fight."

"Your brother," the kagan said. "Alp. That's another thing, alas, that I know something about."

"He is not dead," she said. "No. No, he isn't."

"The Rus encountered a plague when they reached Derbent," the kagan said. "Or perhaps the plague was booty they acquired along the way south. They may even, I do not know, have brought it with them out of the North. Some illnesses lie hidden in the body like burrs in a fold of a cloak, for days and weeks and even months, before they flower."

Filaq remembered how her brother looked on the summer day she last saw him, tall and gangly, speaking tenderly to the falcon on his arm, as he rode to hunt at their family's horde amid the plane trees and the cicadas and the wild surge of grapevines in the hills. She looked away so that they would not see her tears, and noticed, on its carved and gilded stand, the giant illuminated Ibn Khordadbeh that had so enchanted her as a child, with its maps and preposterous anatomies and flat-foot descriptions of miracles and wonders, page after page of cities to visit and peoples to live among and selves to invent, out there, beyond the margins of her life, along the roads and in the kingdoms.

"I will help you," the kagan said. "Because I was

fond of your father, at least to a point, and even more because I have always been fond of you. There is nothing now that I can do to help your brother, least of all seat him on the tripod. But I can order Buljan to abdicate. I am a prisoner of my title. But so, though he has yet to be forced to acknowledge it, is he."

"The man wiped out the family of this girl," Amram said. "He executed five hundred of the kaganate's finest troops, mowed them down in cold blood. I suppose I don't need to tell you that."

"True enough," the kagan said.

"It strikes me that conceivably he might therefore behave in whatever way suits his purposes best," the African said. "Regardless of what you tell him to do."

"The bek may not disobey the kagan."

"That is true," she told Amram. "We have had revolution and coup and civil war now and then in our history. But that is one thing we have never had."

"He ignored your own flag of truce," Zelikman said.

"True, and yet I think he will go," the kagan said. "Palace life does not hold the appeal for Buljan that he imagined it would. But first, you see, I must be persuaded to *order* him to go."

"And what is it going to take to make that happen?" Zelikman said.

"It's really quite simple," the kagan said. "I just want you to kill me."

A silence ensued, during which the partners conferred wordlessly, stroking their chins while she watched, fidgeting and stalking the circular room, wanting to look at the book she had loved but afraid that if she did she would never be able to live with the paltry self that fortune had chosen for her.

"We can do that," Amram said to the kagan.

"We can?" Zelikman said, looking less startled than interested by his partner's claim.

"Of course. I already beat Buljan once at shatranj with the sacrifice. I hate to waste such a fine chance of doing it to him again."

CHAPTER FOURTEEN

ON THE MELANCHOLY DUTY OF SOLDIERS TO CONTEND WITH THE MESSES LEFT BY KINGS

After a hasty mutual debriefing, the guards, groggy and sheepish and lacking a full complement of ears, roused an old Wendish manservant and sent him into the tower to find out the worst. The Wend, sightless and mute, knew the proper smells and bodily utterances of his man and the circular echoes of the apartment so well that on reaching it he could hear the books that had been moved from their right places, and his sapient nostrils at once discerned the intrusive brackish smell of river water and a faint ribbon of some rank attar in the air. He covered his face with his hands and sank to the floor by the couch that was covered in the hide of a spotted tarpan, and silently wept. He had been born a bondsman into a family of slaves, and his life was bondage, and in that regard he counted himself no worse than the general run of humanity, not excluding his master, who was the slave of an exacting God and in this nowhere near so fortunately owned as the Wend.

After a little while the Wend got up and wiped his face on his sleeve, and made a study of the angles, likelihoods and protocols of the business at hand. He dragged a Tabriz carpet from the floor and, with a muttered apology, threw it over the mass whose smell of bitter asphodel and silent bulk freighted the couch. He tucked one end of the carpet under this side of the body, careful not to allow even the tips of his fingernails to brush against the flesh, lest he be pursued through the fogbound eternity of his Wendish ancestors by the misplaced and revenging shade of his master, heaved the great bulk to the floor and rolled the dead emperor up in the Tabriz rug, leaving a long flap at the head and feet to facilitate lifting.

While the soldiers worked the body down the spiral stair, the Wend made the long, slow ascent to the turret, carrying a leather pouch tucked under his arm. When he reached the top and stood in the wind he took out a triangular white flag marked with a red rune, unfolded it and hoisted it from the standard, beneath the candelabrum flag of the empire; and thus, against a bright gray sky, with the first fat flakes of snow drifting all around, was the news published to the world that Zachariah, the kagan of the Khazars, had been the victim of a foul assassination.

This faithful Wend was the one who, woken earlier in the night by an urgent pealing of his master's bell, had conveyed from the tower apartment to the quarters of the messenger corps three sealed copies of a written fiat, to be delivered at once to the bek, to the kender and to the grand rabbi of Atil. The couriers sent to the central barracks where the kender was quartered and to the home of the grand rabbi discharged their commissions and returned to their billet in the Palace, but the messenger charged with bringing Buljan the demand for his immediate abdication had a more difficult job, and by the time he tracked Buljan down, on the low reddish hill called Qizl at the southern extreme of Atil, it was nearly the third hour after dawn, and by then Buljan had other concerns.

At first light, around the time that the body of the kagan—a body that had already begun to manifest decidedly uncorpselike signs of movement—was being carried by an ill-assorted trio into a springhouse near a little-used gate of the Palace through which corpses and those who tended to them traditionally passed, the watch posted atop Qizl caught sight of a scattering of black seeds against the flickering gray of the southern horizon. At first the seeds drifted nearly motionless as milkweed pouf but as they blew nearer they cut long, slow grooves in the water. They grew wings and sprouted brazen necks that seemed to reach devouring toward Atil, like eels contending from a tidepool for a castoff morsel on a rock. The ships' sails bellied and swung about on the spars as they drove against the north wind, cutting a zigzag course. By the third hour, when the breathless messenger at last found the bek and transmitted the sealed order, two dozen long ships were rounding the headland on whose summit Buljan stood in the falling snow, waiting to see if—as every other soul on Qizl, along the river, watching from the walls of the city hoped—the Northmen meant to sail on. News of the death of the kagan had sped across the city after the hoisting of the rune flag, accompanied in an imperial style by a retinue of rumors that the Rus, the Muslims or the bek himself were responsible.

Buljan was trying to decide just what it was that he hoped for as he tore open the seal on the final command of Zachariah. He conned the document without displaying interest or distress. He turned to the javshigar who stood by his side, a captain of archers in a scale-mail coat.

"Signal the ships," he told the javshigar, motioning

He turned to the javshigar who stood by his side, a captain
of archers in a scale-mail coat.

to a scribe for a tablet and stylus. "I want to parley with Ragnar, if he is still in command of them." With the stylus and with an urgency that betrayed his calm expression he pressed a series of runes into the wax of the tablet. "If not, then whoever keeps those yellow dogs leashed." He handed the tablet back to the scribe and told him, "Take this to the bekun." Then he mounted his horse and sent it at a canter down the hill toward the Caspian wharfs.

As the remnant of that giant fleet—launched at midsummer from the viks of the North to fatten, with Buljan's full consent and encouragement, on the Muhammadan cities of southern Khazaria—returned to the mouth of the river they called Volga, the Northmen richer and covered in glory but their ranks thinned by plague and battle and an appalling toll of alcoholism, the army of Khazaria was completing its long homeward tramp to Atil. Having reduced three Crimean cities and brought their populations back under the candelabrum flag, the Khazar army found itself obliged to abandon its campaign in the rebellious Crimea, summoned home by an urgent appeal from Buljan: a Muhammadan uprising, northern cities swooning like maidens at the feet of a boy general and his army of peasants. Though scouts had since brought back reports of the rebellion's collapse, the total absence of any trace of disturbance surprised the tarkhan of the Crimean force now as he urged his horse down from the hills along the road that ran east toward the city. All around Atil lay only a great silent waste, dotted with silver marsh and green scrub and devoid of men or horses. He could see plumes of smoke rising up from the Khazaran side that must be remnant of the rioting that his scouts had reported, but they were few and thin. Unless the rioters themselves had gained control of and pacified Atil, there would be little employment for his troops here, and their frantic homeward march across a hundred leagues of forest and desert and steppe a fruitless journey, futile at either end. The falling snow, twisting in lazy helices to settle in streaks and patches on the plain, seemed both to embody and to enhance the pointlessness of the haste and fury with which he had driven his troops over the last week. Politics, cowardice and the corrupt broils of leadership had spoiled the campaign, and the tarkhan with the romantic pessimism of old veterans felt the missed opportunity, in his bones, as one that would never again present itself to the Khazars. There was no hope for an empire that lost the will to prosecute the grand and awful business of adventure.

His melancholy reflections were interrupted by the return of his aide-de-camp, his broad Bulgar face tight with suppressed information, from a quick trip up to the front of the column.

"A caravan," the Bulgar said. "Radanite, by the look of them."

A quarter of a league on, where the road finally abandoned the hills for the plain of Atil, a modest train of horses and wagons became entangled with the main body of the Crimean force, and the tarkhan dismounted and approached the lead Radanite wagon, a monstrous thing of heavy timber with tenoned wheels nearly as tall as the tarkhan drawn by two teams of massive, humped oxen, shaggy as wisents. It was driven by a young trader with a foolish way of smiling. On one side of him sat a rawhide-faced old mummy, thin and dark, with eyes as charitable as an eagle's. On the other side of the witless-looking driver a huge, fat Radanite with an unaccountably regal bearing beamed down, his pudding of a face so suffused with smugness or pleasure that the tarkhan immediately suspected the caravan of smuggling, or duty evasion, then dismissed the suspicion, knowing that none of their ilk would ever make such an arrant display of mercantile subterfuge. Next it struck him that this cheerful imperiousness might itself be a kind of subterfuge, and he ordered the contents of the wagon unloaded and checked against the bills of lading and the tax warrants from the customs house of Atil.

"Your excellency will naturally find that all of our documents are in order," the old mummy said. "Though obtaining them at all was a considerable feat, given the turmoil that prevails in the Palace this morning."

Thus the tarkhan and his army learned of the death of the kagan. He ordered his troops to dismount and face the Palace, and there was a loud rush as of wind over thick grasses as they knelt in the road, their armor creaking, and prostrated themselves on the dense, half-frozen ground.

"Very sad," said the great fat Radanite, giving his cheeks a rueful shake. "Tragic, really."

The tarkhan gave the order for a halt while he had a fire built and sat the merchants around it. He questioned them at length and in his mounting urgency and confusion failed, perhaps, to remark that his interlocutors were offering information, speculation and unfounded hearsay in a style that ill befitted and was hardly characteristic of Radanites. The snowflakes fell into the fire with an endless chorus of derisive hissing, and as the snow settled on the soldiers and the wagons and the rattling leaves of the boxwood trees, and as the

Radanites concluded their testimony to the perfidy and outrages committed by the stooge and lackey Buljan, there presented itself to the tarkhan the odious question of what he ought to do next. Though he despised and misunderstood politics he was accustomed to wading through it as, when pressing an attack, through the slick of gore underfoot. Word of the massacre of the Arsiyah was already passing in half-whispers through his army, among whom there were many Muhammadan troopers. Treachery, regicide, rebellion; and a week's march behind him a Crimean city left ripe and unchastened. And meanwhile this great wisent of a Radanite blandly suggesting, with all due respect, and as if this were anything but the most unwelcome observation in the history of generalship, that the future of the kaganate might well lie in his capable hands.

"Who is that?" said the old mummy, rising slowly to his feet. The tarkhan turned and saw three riders coming up the road from the city. One was a young man, dressed in thick leggings, quilted Greek tunic and stained leather armor of the sort worn by the Rus, but with the face and the unmistakable green eyes of a Khazar. The others were a giant black man and a thin pale fellow, dressed in tattered oddments of armor and rag. The big one's eyes conducted what the general recognized as a professional assessment of their size, arms and mettle without betraying any hint of his conclusions, and the thin one bothered only to look politely scornful as if he found the whole idea of armies a bore. The young one rode right up to the tarkhan, whose hand went to his sword. The green eyes stirred a memory in the tarkhan, of the smell of linden flowers maddening the twilight on the eve of the Battle of Balanjar, in a meadow above a deep gorge from which there issued the distant boom of a river, and of the green-eyed bek who had inspired his commanders that night with a song of the hero Dede Korkut. He let go of the hilt of his sword.

"You know me," said the young man.

"I know you," the tarkhan said, not quite convinced.

"You held me on your knee, Chorpan," the young man said. "You told me a story about my namesake, Alp Er, and the wolf. You gave me a bow of horn, yes? Now I and my friends have slipped the chains that bound us to the rowing benches of the Rus, and come up from the river to find you."

"To what end?"

"To assume command of this army," said the young man, "and avenge all the crimes that Buljan has committed."

The general heard something in this Alp's voice that he did not fully credit, and saw something in the face that he wanted to believe. He turned from the familiar gaze of the young man to a consideration of his soldiers, who had risen to their feet and stood watching the scene between their general and a beardless stripling with studied and sullen disinterest. Perhaps their desire to live another day outweighed their thirst for battle, but if you added to the latter their abhorrence of doing nothing at all, the balance tipped. For his part he wanted nothing more than to exercise his heart and right arm and leave all questions of credit and belief, of consideration and desire, to others who would do with them what they would, whether men died or generals or empires.

"I confess that I'm intrigued by your proposition, not to mention your audacity," the tarkhan said. "But I feel constrained to point out that in fact it was a bow of ash wood, not horn."

The young man blinked. The thin, pale rider coughed into his fist, and tried not quite successfully to conceal his amusement. The giant's horse bumped as if by chance against the horse of the green-eyed young man, jarring him out of his hesitation.

"My mistake," said the stripling.

CHAPTER FIFTEEN

ON FOLLOWING THE ROAD TO ONE'S DESTINY, WITH THE USUAL INTRUSIONS OF VIOLENCE AND GRACE

For half a day the captain of archers—a javshigar in the Army of the Khazar with fifteen years of service to the candelabrum flag—had suffered, shifting from foot to foot, pulling now at his mustache, now at the fingers of his glove, as the warrior king to whom he had sworn loyalty by oaths so ancient and binding they resisted even the power of the autumnal Disavowal haggled and pleaded for the safety of the house of Buljan with a barbarous swaggering Rus butcher whom the vicissitudes of the plunderous life had left only half a face.

Then as in ages to come it was a point of contention whether the Northmen were better endowed by their greedy and termagant gods for commerce or slaughter, but in the judgment of the captain of archers these were complementary gifts. Hour after hour the two men dickered, the bek with his wife at his side, his children squalling or staring in dumb wonder at the Rus. The Northmen sprawled along the wharf like white mountains in bloodstained tunics, encouraging Ragnar Half-Face to turn the greasy Khazar upside down by the ankles and shake him until every last dirham fell out of his pockets. Around them long trains of Buljan's slaves staggered down from the Qomr with armloads and sacks of gold and silver plate, gemstones and ivory, silks and spices and perfumed wood, making up the price of passage for Buljan and his household. The Rus rowed the booty out to their ships and then rowed back again blowing and grinning and hungry for more. The captain of archers fidgeted and coughed and rolled his eyes at his men, as if such cupidity and dishonor were an inevitable but minor aspect of the human predicament akin to sharptonguedness in a wife, but felt a hot needle of outrage sounding his belly. He prayed to his own God of Outrage, Iehovah, to send a righteous thunderbolt to strike the half-leering Rus chieftain down or, at the very least, to satisfy the bastard, and once and for all rid Khazaria of the stain of cowardice and the smell of the Northmen and of the ruinous usurper Buljan. But when the captain saw them bring-

ing down the new elephant and felt the thrill of dismay
running through all the stout Khazar archers of his
company, he felt the insufficiency of prayer to the relief
of grievous outrage. He settled his armored cap more
firmly on his head, and cleared his throat, and with a
hand on the hilt of his Damascene poniard strode heels
knocking against the dock over to the side of the man
who in a show of bankrupt bravery had proclaimed
himself bek, and lowering his eyes, his voice clear but
his manner as yet tinged with the long habit of obedi-
ence, said,

"I regret, honored Buljan, that I must place you
under arrest."

At once all the Northmen got up and unsheathed
their blades or spoke eager promises to their axes.
There were at least two hundred of them, and though
rumor had described them as flux-ridden and liver-
sore and spent, they were now in possession of a kingly
treasure, with the promise of an elephant and a chance
of bloodshed, and looking fresher and gayer by the instant. The archer had his twenty men, their shooting
skill blunted at close range, their daggers inadequate.
High up on the walls of the city another company of
archers looked down, fine marksmen all and as prone
to outrage at the scandal of the looting of the elephant,
but their grasp of the situation at a bowshot was no

doubt limited. Meanwhile, the bek's personal body-guards, thick-skulled glowering Colchians, owned impenetrable minds and loyalty only to their paymaster.

"Must you," Buljan said in a distracted way, watching the magnificent old animal swing down the ramp with its womanly gait, ringing like gongs the sawed planks each as thick as a strong man's wrist. When the captain had last seen the beast she was caparisoned and painted like a whore at carnival, but now she came wearing nothing but the rich gray terrain of her hide, scarred and dignified and so replete with power in the shifting under the skin of her monstrous musculature that she seemed to the captain to embody the antiquity and might of the kaganate—and in her imminent journey from the embankment to the barge that stood waiting to tow her up the river to the home of the Northmen, where she would surely perish in the cold and the dark, that empire's passing. "I wonder how?"

And Buljan drew his own short sword and before the captain of archers could flinch or turn heaved it up into the soft exposed region just under the captain's arm. There was no pain, at first, only heat and the rank breath of Buljan whistling through his teeth, and an unbearable sadness, and then one of the Northmen laughed as the captain sat down on the dock, and then it hurt. The Rus moved in a boiling tangle like a troop of murderous monkeys the captain had once seen ravaging a village, far away to the southeast in Hind, and his men unsheathed their daggers, and the captain closed his eyes. To his great surprise his death was accompanied or heralded by the sounding of ram's horns, which struck him as a little showy, perhaps, and then there was a silence that accorded more with his expectations, and he opened his eyes and saw his men standing with daggers ready and the Northmen milling, shoulders together and sullen-eyed like boys caught at mischief. From the shore there came a coin-chink of stirrup and mail and harness bit, chiming over and over like some kind of bellicose carillon, and he turned and saw an army, the army, his army, wave after wave of riders and footmen pouring and clattering onto the embankment and filling in every inch of space between the wharves and the walls of the city. And in their midst or at the head of them rode a slender young man with head erect and mouth full and scornful.

He rode down the ramp and as he passed the elephant, reached up to stroke her flank. He reined his horse by the captain of archers and looked down, a beautiful young man, breathing hard like a green recruit about to make his first bloody charge.

"Are you all right?" he said to the captain of the guard.

"I may well die," said the captain of archers, feeling as grateful for the sight of the young man as for a cold drink of water. And in fact the youth now threw down a waterskin, with a solemn nod. Then he leapt from the back of his horse and rushed at Buljan the usurper without warning or art, chopping with his sword as if it were an ax. It was an ugly move, and Buljan, who was among the best swordsmen of his people and generation, easily ducked it and sidestepped. The sword came whistling down and lodged with a discordant twang in the timber of the dock, and while the youth struggled to free its edge from the grip of the hard wood Buljan leaned forward, peering curiously at the face of the young man, and then catching hold of the youth and wrapping his long arms around him did something that struck the captain of archers, and no doubt every soul animal or human on the wharf that afternoon, as strange: he smelled him.

"You," he said, dismayed or delighted, it was hard to say. The youth struggled, kicking and squirming and trying to reach around with his teeth and bite at Buljan, but the usurper held him easily and fast. He laughed a false laugh that held genuine bitterness, and turned to the army that watched motionless from the shore. "This is your new bek?" he called out. And he unsheathed his own dagger now and held it to the fine young throat. "This is no bek. This is the mother of a bek. She carries my seed in her belly!"

The dagger flashed and his arm came up. It never came down. A thick gray vine snaked down and took hold of it and, like a Rus ceremoniously killing off an amphora of wine, hoisted Buljan into the air and brought him down against the dock. The breath huffed from Buljan's lungs and certain of his bones could be heard to break, and he lay there stunned, and no thing but the river moved or made a sound. Then Buljan's wife screamed as the elephant laced its trunk around his ankles, hoisted him again into the air and slammed him down once more, ensuring the fracture of skull and vertebrae. The elephant appeared to enjoy the business and repeated it several more times, and when the captain of archers at last averted his gaze from the mass of pulp and leather he saw that a ghostly scarecrow clad in black had appeared behind the twin daughters of Buljan to blindfold their faces with his long white fingers. At last the elephant lost interest or took pity and dragged the broken body across the timbers, leaving a bloody trail, to lay it—with a tenderness in which a sentimental man might infer a note of apology—at the feet of the widow of Buljan.

The youth rose shakily to his feet and raised his sword and turned, slowly, around and around. By now the Rus were scrambling into the barge intended for the transport of the elephant, showing considerable alacrity and even a cowardly grace. The youth pointed to Ragnar Half-Face, who in his haste to flee had stumbled over several bolts of fine blue silk of Khitai, and a big man with skin the color of tarnished copper ran after him, surprisingly fleet for a gray-hair, and caught the Rus chieftain, and dragged him back to face the young man.

"Who are you?" Ragnar said.

"I am Alp," said the young man, and the captain of archers knew him then, recalled from some parade or guard detail the piercing green eyes of the boy's mother's people.

"You are not Alp," Ragnar said. "You resemble him. But Alp died puking blood over the side of my ship, chained to a rowing bench."

The youth reached for his sword, but now the pale hand of the scarecrow shot out and took hold of the young man's wrist.

"Enough," he said.

"You will die a far more unpleasant death still," said the dark-skinned giant, "unless you return all that you have looted from the shores of this sea."

The giant pushed him to his knees, and Ragnar looked down, his greasy yellow braids tumbling around his face. Then he looked up again with a mercantile glint, his half-face twisted as if in wry pleasure, looking from the pale man to the dark.

"What a pair of swindlers!" he said admiringly. "Gentlemen of the road, hustling a kingdom! Who are you?"

But if any reply was made to this question, the captain of archers never heard it.

That night Zelikman and Amram welcomed the Sabbath in the dosshouse on Sturgeon Street, with Hanukkah and Sarah and Flower of Life and a number of infidel whores who saw no greater harm in marking the sacred time of the country than in accommodating the needs of its men. The women and men alike covered their heads and hid their faces behind their hands and blessed the light. When the candles had burned down and the first of the night's clients—foreigners, sailors, Christians and the lapsed—had arrived, Amram took to a bedroom with Flower of Life. One by one everyone got up from the table and went through the curtain to work, leaving Zelikman and Hanukkah alone.

"Where will you go?" Hanukkah said.

"I am the great sage who suggested we try the road

"What a pair of swindlers!" he said admiringly.

from the Black Sea to the Caucasus," Zelikman said. "It's his turn to choose."

"I could come with you," Hanukkah said, pulling at his pudgy chin as if trying out the idea on himself.

Zelikman reached over and patted him on the knee. "You have a woman to redeem," he said.

"And no gold to redeem her with."

"Come with me," Zelikman said, and they wound down the crooked hall behind the common room, to a small chamber, hardly larger than a privy, in which Zelikman planned to spend the night, not willing to spoil his own melancholy or with it the pleasure of Amram. He opened one of his leather bags and took out a sack of dirhams mixed with gold scudi and Greek coin that represented about half the payment he had received for his services to the new bek of Khazaria, and handed it to Hanukkah.

"I doubt she's worth half that," he said irritably. "Now go away and leave me alone. I wish to sulk."

Hanukkah embraced him and kissed him, his breath vinous and his emotion nettlesome to Zelikman, who sent the little bandit on his way with a kick in the seat of his breeches. Then Zelikman knelt on the floor beside his cot and passed an hour inventorying and consolidating his herbiary and pharmakon, thinking about his father, away in the stone and fog of Regensburg, and how he would interpret or respond to the abject, heartfelt, even florid letter of apology and recantation that the leathern old Radanite had extracted from Zelikman as payment for allowing first him and then the kagan to pose as one of them. When his gear was packed he took out his pipe and the last of his bhang. For a long time he sat, listening to the barking of dogs and to the sad fiddling of the rebab, thin and plaintive in the snowy air, with the flint and striker in his hand. He was about to light the pipe when he heard a footstep outside his door. He reached for Lancet but she slipped into the room before he could get his fingers around the hilt. She had come to him as a girl, in a long wool skirt and a wool coat, hood trimmed with spotted fur. There was snow on her eyelashes and on the fur trim and about her an iron smell of snow. He stood, and they looked at each other, and then stepped quickly together as if stealing an embrace against the coming of an enemy or a watchful governess.

"I have never kissed a woman before," he confessed to her when they parted again.

"A man?"

He shook his head.

"Now you have accomplished both at once," she said. "Quite a feat."

"I would invite you to share my bed," Zelikman said. "But it is a poor one, and I fear that I would acquit myself very poorly in it."

"My standard of comparison is so low," she said. "The fact that I'm actually consenting to it may compensate for your absence of technique."

"I understand," he said.

They took off their clothes, and climbed under the thin blanket, and warmed their hands in the darkness at the little fire they made. He verified, too quickly at first, that she was indeed female in all her particulars, and both of them were contented, for the moment, with that.

"Will you go to Africa?" she asked him.

"Maybe," Zelikman said. "Filaq, ride with us. With me. Follow the roads, see the kingdoms." He took hold of her again, improving somewhat upon his first performance. She stroked his hair and ran her hand along the cheek that he had shaved smooth of its bogus Radanite beard.

"That isn't my true name, by the way," she said. "Filaq."

"Will you tell me your true name?"

"Only if you promise not to ask me to come with you," she said.

"I promise."

She paused, as if for effect, and then looked straight into his eyes.

"My name is Alp," she said. "I am the bek and kagan of Khazaria."

He was disappointed, but he felt the foolishness of that disappointment, and like a vial of tincture that had lost its volatility he put it aside.

"Oho," he said. "Bek *and* kagan."

"The current system has become unwieldy."

"Swindler!" Zelikman said, knowing as he kissed her that no one would ever touch her as a woman again. "Hustling a kingdom."

In the morning when Zelikman woke she had gone, taking the knowledge of her true name with her. He went to rouse Amram, but his partner had already re-moved himself from the warm bed of Flower of Life and stood waiting in the yard, in a wolfskin cloak and a cloud of breath from the horses, stamping his feet, complaining of the chill in bones that were too old for love and for adventure and for dragging his African ass halfway around the world all on account of elephants.

"Do you want to stay?" Zelikman said, looking up at a high small window cut into the stone wall, where Flower of Life now leaned, chin in hand, her face giving nothing away.

Amram swung up onto the back of Porphyrogene,

and flicked the reins, and that was all the answer that he gave. And then they took the first road that led out of the city, unmindful of whether it turned east or south, their direction a question of no interest to either of them, their destination already intimately known, each of them wrapped deep in his thick fur robes and in the solitude that they had somehow contrived to share.

AFTERWORD

The original, working—and in my heart the true—title of the short novel you hold in your hands was *Jews with Swords*.

When I was writing it, and happened to tell people the name of my work in progress, it made them want to laugh. I guess it seemed clear that I meant the title as a joke. It has been a very long time, after all, since Jews anywhere in the world routinely wore or wielded swords, so long that when paired with "sword," the word "Jews" (unlike, say, "Englishmen" or "Arabs") clangs with anachronism, with humorous incongruity, like "Samurai Tailor" or *Santa Claus Conquers the Martians*. True, Jewish soldiers fought in the blade-era battles of Austerlitz and Gettysburg; notoriously, Jewish boys were stolen from their families and conscripted into the czarist armies of nineteenth-century Russia. Any of those fighting men, or any of the Jews who served in the armed forces, particularly in the cavalry units, of their homelands prior to the end of WWI might have qualified, I suppose, as Jews with swords.

But hearing the title, nobody seemed to flash on the image of doomed Jewish troopers at Inkerman, Antietam, or the Somme, or of dueling Arabized courtiers at Muslim Granada, or even, say, on the memory of some ancient warrior Jew, like Bar Kochba or Judah Maccabee, famed for his prowess at arms. They saw, rather, an unprepossessing little guy, with spectacles and a beard, brandishing a sabre: the pirate Motel Kamzoil. They pictured Woody Allen backing toward the nearest exit behind a barrage of wisecracks and a wavering rapier. They saw their uncle Manny, dirk between his teeth, slacks belted at the armpits, dropping from the chandelier to knock together the heads of a couple of nefarious auditors.

And, okay, so maybe I didn't look very serious when I told people the title. Yet I meant it sincerely, or half-sincerely; or maybe it would be more accurate to say that I could not have entitled this book any more honestly than by means of anachronism and incongruity.

I know it still seems incongruous, first of all, for me

or a writer of my literary training, generation, and pre-
tensions to be writing stories featuring *anybody* with
swords. As recently as ten years ago I had published
two novels, and perhaps as many as twenty short stories, and not one of them featured weaponry more an-
tique than a (lone) Glock 9mm. None was set any
earlier than about 1972 or in any locale more far-flung
or exotic than a radio studio in Paris, France. Most of
those stories appeared in sedate, respectable, and gen-
erally sword-free places like *The New Yorker* and *Harper's*,
and featured unarmed Americans undergoing the eter-
nal fates of contemporary short-story characters—
disappointment, misfortune, loss, hard enlightenment,
moments of bleak grace. Divorce; death; illness; violence, random and domestic; divorce; bad faith; decep-
tion and self-deception; love and hate between fathers
and sons, men and women, friends and lovers; the
transience of beauty and desire; divorce—I guess that
about covers it. Story, more or less, of my life. As for the
two novels, they didn't stray in time or space any farther than the stories—or for that matter, any deeper
into the realm of Jewishness: both set in Pittsburgh,
liberally furnished with Pontiacs and Fords, scented
with marijuana, Shalimar and kielbasa, featuring
Smokey Robinson hits and *Star Trek* references, and
starring gentiles or assimilated Jews, many of whom

were self-consciously inspired, instructed and laid low by the teachings of rock and roll and Hollywood, but not, for example, by the lost writings of the *tzaddík* of Regensburg, whose commentaries are so important to one of the heroes of *Gentlemen of the Road*.

I'm not saying—let me be clear about this—I am not saying that I disparage or repudiate my early work, or the genre (late-century naturalism) it mostly exemplifies. I am proud of stories like "House Hunting," "S Angel," "Werewolves in Their Youth," and "Son of the Wolfman," and out of all my novels I may always be most fond of *Wonder Boys*, which saved my life, kind of, or saved me, at least, from having to live in a world in which I must forever be held to account for the doomed second novel it supplanted. I'm not turning my back on the stuff I wrote there, late in the twentieth century, and I hope that readers won't either. It's just that here, in *Gentleman of the Road* as in some of its recent predecessors, you catch me in the act of trying, as a writer, to do what many of the characters in my earlier stories—Art Bechstein, Grady Tripp, Ira Wiseman— were trying, longing, ready to do: I have gone off in search of a little adventure.

If this impulse seems an incongruous thing in a writer of the ("serious," "literary") kind for which I had for a long time hoped to be taken, it might be explained—as I think the enduring popularity of all adventure fiction might be explained—with simple reference to the kind of *person* I am. I have never swung a battle-ax or a sword. I have never, thank God, killed anybody. I have never served as a soldier of empire or fortune, infiltrated a palace or an enemy camp in the dead of night, or ridden an elephant, though I have— barely, and without the least confidence or style— ridden a horse. I do not laugh in the face of death and danger; far from it. I have never survived in the desert on a few swallows of acrid water and a handful of scorched millet. Never escaped from prison, the gallows or the rowing benches of a swift caravel. Never gambled my life and fortune on a single roll of the dice; if I lose $100 at a Las Vegas craps table, it makes me feel like crying.

This is not to say that I have never had adventures: I have had my fill and more of them. Because adventures befall the unadventuresome as readily, if not as frequently, as the bold. Adventures are a logical and reliable result—and have been since at least the time of Odysseus—of the fatal act of leaving one's home, or trying to return to it again. All adventure happens in that damned and magical space, wherever it may be found or chanced upon, which least resembles one's home. As soon as you have crossed your doorstep or the county line, into that place where the structures, laws, and conventions of your upbringing no longer apply, where the support and approval (but also the disapproval and repression) of your family and neighbors are not to be had: then you have entered into adventure, a place of sorrow, marvels, and regret. Given a choice, I very much prefer to stay home, where I may safely encounter adventure in the pages of a book, or seek it out, as I have here, at the keyboard, in the friendly wilderness of my computer screen.

I guess what I'm trying to say is that if there is incongruity in the writer of a piece of typical *New Yorker* marital-discord fare like "That Was Me" (a story in my second collection) turning out a swords-and-horses tale like this one, it's nothing compared to the incongruous bounty to be harvested from the actual sight of me sitting on a horse, for example, or trying to keep from falling out of a whitewater raft, or setting off, as I have done from time to time with sinking heart and in certainty of failure but goaded into wild hopefulness by some treacherous friend or bold stranger, in search of a Springsteenian something in the night.

This incongruity of writer and work suggests, of course, that classic variant of the adventure story (found in works as diverse as *Don Quixote* and *Romancing the Stone*) in which a devoted reader or author of the stuff is granted the opportunity (or obliged) to live out an adventure "in real life." And it is seen in this light that the association of Jews with swords, of Jews with adventure, may seem paradoxically less incongruous. In the relation of the Jews to the land of their origin, in the ever-extending, ever-thinning cord, braided from the freedom of the wanderer and the bondage of exile, that binds a Jew to his Home, we can make out the unmistakable signature of adventure. The story of the Jews centers around—one might almost say that it *stars*—the hazards and accidents, the misfortunes and disasters, the feats of inspiration, the travail and despair, and intermittent moments of glory and grace, that entail upon journeys from home and back again. For better and worse it has been one long adventure—a five-thousand-year Odyssey—from the moment of the true First Commandment, when God told Abraham *lech lecha:* Thou shalt leave home. Thou shalt get lost. Thou shalt find slander, oppression, opportunity, escape, and destruction. Thou shalt, by definition, find adventure. This long, long tradition of Jewish adventure may look a bit light on the Conans or D'Artagnans; our greatest heroes less obviously suited to exploits of derring-do and arms. But maybe that ill-suitedness only makes Jews all the more ripe to feature in (or to write) this kind of tale. Or maybe it is time to take a look backward at that tradition, as I have attempted to do here, and find some shadowy kingdom where a self-respecting Jewish adventurer would not be caught dead without his sword or his battle-ax.

And if you still think there's something funny in the idea of Jews with swords, look at yourself, right now: sitting in your seat on a jet airplane, let's say, in your unearthly orange polyester and neoprene shoes, listening to digital music, crawling across the sky from Charlotte to Las Vegas, and hoping to lose yourself—your home, your certainties, the borders and barriers of your life—by means of a bundle of wood pulp, sewn and glued and stained with blobs of pigment and resin. *People with Books.* What, in 2007, could be more incongruous than that? It makes me want to laugh.

—*Michael Chabon*

MICHAEL CHABON

Michael Chabon is the author of *The Mysteries of
Pittsburgh*; *Wonder Boys*, which was made into a critically
acclaimed film; *The Amazing Adventures of Kavalier & Clay*, which
won the Pulitzer Prize; *The Final Solution: A Story of Detection*;
and *The Yiddish Policemen's Union*. He is also the author of
two collections of short stories and a young adult novel,
Summerland. He lives in the San Francisco Bay area.